IT'S TOO LATE TO
DIE YOUNG NOW

Gary R. Hope

"It's Too Late to Die Young Now" by Gary R. Hope ISBN 978-1-62137-745-0 (softcover); 978-1-62137-746-7 (eBook).

Published 2015 by Virtualbookworm.com Publishing Inc., P.O. Box 9949, College Station, TX, 77842, US.

Dedicated to:
My mom, who deserved more from life
My wife, who deserves everything from life
My sister, who challenges and loves life
My daughter, who needs to understand the meaning of life
My niece, who is living the life
and
My granddaughter, who is life

Table of Contents

PREFACE

I used to think I was a good man. But now I know that was just an illusion, a way of fooling myself. A way of rationalizing my life and the decisions I made throughout the years. As I lie here, with a few weeks , or if I'm lucky, a few months left to live; I need to relieve myself of the guilt I've carried around for most of my 73 years. I can't undo the hurt both known and unknown, that my actions have caused so many people. The only thing I can do now is confess my transgressions and admit I've not been a good person. Most people think I have been good, that I've led a nice life. That I've treated people fairly, been loyal, been trustworthy, honest and faithful. I have not. I, George Winston Kerry, have been a scoundrel, a cheat, a liar and a grand illusionist—making people see something in me that I am not.

What is bringing out this confessional now? Cancer. The end is near and I want to set the record straight. I have the most embarrassing of all cancers (in my opinion), rectal cancer. Yes, this awful disease is killing me from my butt. When I've had to tell people what was wrong with me, they all look concerned and rightfully so. But, inside I know they want to grin, thinking "cancer of the butt?" Well, it is that, it starts in your butt, but just like all cancers, it just keeps growing, spreading and devouring anything and everything in its way, until your body cannot fight it any longer—as is my case.

The doctors tell me it won't be long and there is nothing else that can be done. All the treatments have done is prolong my life by several months and cause me pain and sickness enduring it all— which I truly deserve by the way. I am not bemoaning my fate, not wondering "Why me?" In fact, I often wonder why something like this hasn't happened to me sooner.

I never really took care of myself, nor exercised with any consistency. I never paid any attention to my diet, except that I tried not to get too fat, but I always ate what I wanted to. I only went to see doctors when I was sick, never for checkups, and for close to 73 years this formula worked. I'm not going to tell anyone to start exercising, or to stop eating this or that, or go to the doctor for checkups regularly. Most people don't want to hear any of that.

I mostly think that when it's your time, then it's your time. It really doesn't matter how fit you are when cancer strikes. All you can do at that point is try and fight back, in my case, not very successfully. I was going on vacation (by myself) and just didn't feel well. When I got to my hotel and went to the bathroom I was shocked that my urine was blood red—I knew that was not good.

I tried to stay for a few days, but I just felt terrible, so I cut my stay short and flew back home—if you can call living alone, a home. The doctor sent me to the hospital to confirm what he probably already knew, and after several tests and procedures they confirmed the grim news. What do you do when you hear this news? Call your spouse? Your family? Your friends? What do you do when you're me? I went to an Irish bar and had a drink at 11:00 in the morning and thought of everything in the world that was important to me. It was a short list. At that point in your life, it's amazing how your thoughts can be focused into one or two things that really matter.

This will surprise a lot of people I'm sure, but I truly believe in God. In fact, I talk to Him often, especially when I'm in trouble. I've often wondered why and how I got away with all the stuff I did for so many years. Why I wasn't punished for hurting the people I loved and taking advantage of people I barely knew? I don't know the answers to these questions.

I'm sure God had a plan for me, I'm also sure I disappointed Him, as I did myself. And now that I'm going to meet Him face–to–face, I don't know how I'm going to explain myself. This is scary! I don't want to spend eternity in hell, but how can someone like me ever be admitted into Heaven? Now you understand my dilemma, why I must come clean and confess my wrongs, okay sins...yes they were sins.

My problem, as I rationalize it here, is that I was too smart for my own good. If I hadn't been so smart, maybe I couldn't have figured out how to do the stuff I did and still get away with it. "So George, you're saying its God's fault you did the dastardly things you did? You only did these deeds because He gave you the intelligence to cheat and steal and lie and always get away with it...right?"

Let's wait a bit before I answer that.

I remember taking advantage of my two younger brothers quite often. It was just so darned easy that I couldn't help myself. I don't really think I meant to be mean, it was just a game for me to see what I could get away with and how much they would believe. I would tell them that a coin like a nickel was more valuable than a dime because it was bigger than a dime; and that a penny was more valuable than a dime, because it was bigger. I'd then trade them all my nickels and pennies for their dimes—they thought I was the best big brother ever!

Back in those simple times and days, your parents NEVER asked what you wanted for dinner. Whatever your mom cooked, you ate; or you went hungry. If there was something she prepared that you didn't like, you always had two choices: eat it then with the rest of your dinner, or sit there until you did eat it. No matter how long it took.

I didn't like squash or okra (and I still don't), but it seems we had those two slimy, distasteful vegetables every week—especially in the summer. It didn't matter if I ate it immediately, when it was warm, or if I sat there for a couple of hours until it became cold, oily and slimy, it still tasted horrible.

Our small dining room had a big bay window looking out on the front yard and the street. I always sat in the chair facing the window and made my brothers sit with their backs to the window. I'd get a big spoonful of okra and then point out the window and say, "Who's that kid on the new bike?" Or, "Where does that dog live?" They would both turn around immediately to look out the window and when they did, I'd dump my spoonful of okra on their plate. I never did that in front of dad, he wouldn't have seen the humor in it; but mom would just giggle at my ingenuity. And, I had much less squash and okra to eat...win/win.

In our hallway we had a picture of Jesus, kneeling down in a garden, looking up towards heaven and a light was shining on His face. It was a pretty nice picture and I liked looking at it. I didn't really understand what He was looking at, or why a light was shining on His head, but I enjoyed looking at it. Except when I "exchanged" nickels and pennies for dimes; or dumped food on my brother's plates...I always avoided the hallway then. It was very hard to look at Jesus when I had been a little naughty.

The first act of blatant wrongfulness outside of home, that I remember, was in grade school. We were in the lunch line and I was last in line that day. My good friend Mobley was in front of me eying the fish sticks and English peas the servers were dishing out to us.

Mobley had a very fashionable new wallet in his back pocket, the kind that stuck out of his pocket about half an inch.

Well, I immediately noticed the tip of a $1 bill sticking out the end of his wallet. I looked around—no one was looking at me, no one was behind me. Mobley was talking to Scooter, the class clown, and they were laughing at something—or someone. I grabbed the tip of the $1 bill and quickly snatched it, it came right out. I hadn't planned on stealing Mobley's money, I didn't need the money for anything. The moment just appeared and before you could say "give me two fish sticks please" I had the $1 bill in my pocket and no one knew a thing...except me, and maybe God. I wish I could find Mobley today (if he's still living) and give that dollar back to him. I truly do, that utterly stupid, senseless act has bothered me for over 62 years now.

Why did I steal that money? I liked Mobley, he was my friend, and stayed my friend throughout our school years. Why do any of us do the things we do? Of course I knew better; I knew it was wrong. But the opportunity presented itself and before I knew it, I had done it. The problem was that it was too easy. Maybe if I'd been caught that day 62 years ago, my life would have turned out differently. "So, in effect, you're saying because Mobley didn't catch you that day, it's really his fault you ended up being you...right, George?" Please, conscience, don't give me any outs...I am what I am.

I did little things as a kid that I still remember, things that were wrong that bother me now. Maybe all kids do stuff, I don't know, but I know that I did and now they're coming back to haunt me. My dad would take all the change out of his pockets in the evening when he came home from work and put it all on his dresser in the bedroom. I'd sneak in there and take a dime or a nickel. I'd never take a quarter, I thought he'd miss the quarter, but I didn't think he'd ever miss a nickel or dime. Other times, I could convince my mom that I hadn't had my weekly allowance yet and she would give me my quarter, when in reality, my dad had already given me a quarter. Funny how badly a quarter can make you feel now.

My favorite teacher in school was Ms. Barnett, whom I had in the fifth grade. I don't really know that she was a great teacher or not, but she was very pretty and seemed to like me (more than all the other students, I'm sure). In those grades, you kept the same teacher all day long. She taught English, Math, History, and everything else we took—Ms. Barnett taught it all. I loved Ms. Barnett. When she smiled at a little fifth grader like me, my heart would almost jump out of my body. I'm not really sure if I loved Ms. Barnett like a surrogate mom, or as a fantasy girlfriend. I'd never had a girlfriend before, I didn't know how that felt.

I'd bring Ms. Barnett an apple every week or two. She'd make a big fuss over it. Sometimes I'd save a cupcake that my mom made (if I could hide them from my brothers) and take one to Ms. Barnett.

Thinking back on those cupcakes now, I didn't put them in a baggie, I just wrapped a paper towel around them. I'm pretty sure they were probably stale and hard by the time Ms. Barnett actually had the chance to taste one (if she ever did). But it sure made my little heart skip a beat when she would smile and thank me...I'd do anything for Ms. Barnett. Even steal from her.

Ms. Barnett had this big red pen on her desk at the front of the room that she used to correct our papers. She liked to hold it in her hand as she talked to us and during our lessons...she was always holding it. I often thought that if a magic genie came into my life, I'd like him to change me into that red pen, so Ms. Barnett could hold me all day long. Funny how little kids think.

One day, after lunch, Ms. Barnett told us to put our books away, that it was time for recess. Everyone, excitedly, put their books under their desks, grabbed their coats and hurried outside for a spirited game of kickball, or dodge ball, your choice. I liked dodge ball a lot. It really made my day to hit the bully, Albert, with the ball as hard as I could. It didn't happen often, he usually hit me more than I hit him, but when I did hit him—it was so sweet.

Anyway, this particular day, as I stood up, I noticed my shoe lace was untied, so I stopped to tie it, causing me to be the last student to leave the classroom. As I started to leave, passing next to Ms. Barnett's desk, I saw it...the red pen. It was sitting there, unguarded, seemingly whispering to me, "Take me George, it's okay." I hesitated for an instant, looked around the empty classroom, then I grabbed the pen. I stuck it in my coat jacket and ran outside, feeling exhilarated, scared and guilty for what I'd done.

After recess, when everyone was back in the classroom, Ms. Barnett announced that something had been taken from her desk. She didn't say it was the red pen and she didn't say it was stolen, she said "taken" like someone had borrowed it. She did say she expected whoever took the object, to either put it back on her desk as school ended that day, or to simply leave it somewhere in the classroom so she could find it.

Until that moment, I didn't know it was possible to instantly break out in beads of sweat. I was sure Ms. Barnett would notice how badly I was sweating and that I would be caught. School ended that day. Ms. Barnett didn't catch me. I was by then too scared to put the pen back on her desk, so I took it home. I held the pen that night, but somehow, it didn't make me feel good—in fact, it made me feel bad. I had hurt someone that I loved, I knew right then I was not a good person.

It was a hard, cold fact for an eleven year old to digest. I couldn't stand for the pen to be in my possession any longer, so I threw it in the creek behind our house the next day. I don't know if it was my imagination or not, but I always felt as though Ms. Barnett looked at me differently the rest of the year. I'm pretty sure that's when the little voice in the back of my mind was born.

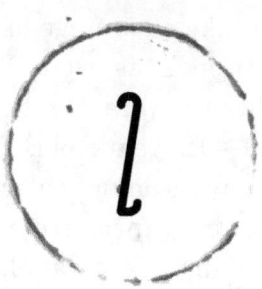

As I got older, my friends and I would meet at a local soda shop to hang out and watch girls. There was a mixed nut display case there with warm, fresh cashews and those nuts smelled so good and looked so inviting. But, they were also very expensive for a kid with no money. I'd look at those nuts every day, smell the sweet aroma of those warm cashews and lust for them on the way home. Oh, how I wished I was rich so I could eat cashews every day!

Soon I began to position myself at the corner of the mixed nut display case and the magazine rack. When everyone was laughing at a joke or looking at a pretty girl who just walked in, I would discreetly lift the lid of the nut case and take 2 or 3 cashews out before anyone knew what had happened. Why did I do this? I wasn't starving. I can't explain it accurately now, just that the temptation overwhelmed me and I could not stop myself. One other time, I bought a comic book and after I paid for it, I slipped another comicbook I hadn't paid for inside the pages of the first one and walked out. How can I remember all these dirty little deeds now, yet not remember birthdays, anniversaries and other important details of my life?

I continued to take advantage of my brothers, and sometimes their friends as well. We loved to play cards. We thought we were big time poker players when we were 11—12 years old. I'd play with my brothers, or we'd have some of their friends over and have up to seven or eight people playing nickel—dime poker. What they didn't know was that I had a built—in advantage. Even then, I was looking for ways where I could benefit at the expense of others.

I saw an ad in a magazine for a "magic" deck of cards that you could do amazing tricks to astound your family and friends. I ordered the "magic cards," not to amaze my family and friends with, but to use for my own personal gain. Each of these "magic" cards had designs on the back that were seemingly all the same. However, each card had a "magic" code that identified that particular card, if you knew how to read the code. That was the "magic" part—being able to understand the code. I could look at the back of each card and tell if it was a 3 of spades, or a king of diamonds. In poker, this ability was an invaluable resource.

Being able to decipher the codes on my "magic" cards gave me the uncanny ability to always have the best hand, or fold if I didn't. My brothers and their friends thought I had the best poker instincts of anyone this side of Wild Bill Hickok! It helps when you know what each card is that your opponent is holding, and what the next card is that's going to be dealt. My amazing poker ability won me a lot of nickels and dimes that summer. It ended when they all refused to play with me anymore, because I always won. So, I took my cards and went home.

In high school I had a job pumping gas at Tom's Texaco. I enjoyed the job and Tom was a good guy to work for. As far as I know he treated all his employees and customers fairly. In those days, in the mid 1950's, us attendants pumped gas in the customer's cars, washed their windshields, checked the oil and the tire pressure. While customers relaxed in their car and drank a 6 oz Coca-Cola while they waited. What simple times they were.

Gas was relatively cheap then, 25-26 cents a gallon. Tom was paying me $1.00 an hour, which was average wages for the day, and I was happy for it. After a few months, the sneakiness in me realized that if a customer got $4.75 worth of regular and paid in cash, I could simply pocket a quarter and put the other $4.50 in the cash register and no one would ever know. Heck, it was only a quarter!

Tom didn't need that quarter, he'd never miss it. Well, maybe not that one quarter, but if I did that three or four times a day, then those quarters added up. I could make an extra dollar a day, and when you're only making $1.00 an hour, an additional dollar a day is a lot of money. I kept rationalizing that old Tom would never miss that "quarter."

I soon began to consider that extra dollar as part of my salary for doing all the dirty work. Like checking the oil and throwing away garbage for customers. Washing their front and back windows, and even checking their tire pressure. Even though I knew what I was doing was wrong, heck, it was only a quarter...right? Tom didn't need it...right George? Sometimes I hate that little voice in the back of my mind. Or was that God talking to me?

Somehow, Tom never found out about the missing quarters and I kept working there when I started college. My hours were flexible and I worked mostly late afternoons and evenings. College life was fun for me, I enjoyed the courses, the interaction and mostly, the parties and the girls. I did fairly well, an "A", a couple of "B"s and a "C" or two in my first year. Honestly, I didn't try very hard and seldom studied at all. I found that if I paid attention during class and listened to the lectures I could usually do okay on the tests and exams.

Some of the courses, like accounting and finance were truly interesting and I was fascinated by the lectures and discussions. Other courses really bored the daylights out of me. Courses like history, sociology and geography were insufferable and it took all my will power just to stay awake during those classes. Interestingly, two courses that intrigued me were Old Testament (first semester) and New Testament (second semester). It seems odd now to be taking religious courses in college. But in those days it was required and we didn't have the ACLU, or any other groups protesting that this was unconstitutional, or some other nonsense.

I thought about taking more religion courses my next year. I was hoping to learn something, not just memorize things from the Bible. That first year, it seems like all we did was memorize the books of the Bible and then recite passages and verses. Never really learning anything, but being tested on how good we could memorize things. Even then, I wanted to see what the Bible was really about and what it had to say to me. However, between the summer of my freshman year and sophomore year, something happened to change my mind.

Our professor, Dr. Henriksonn, who wrote, not only our textbook, but several other texts and books on religion and the Bible, was arrested. It was nothing major, a simple misdemeanor on his part, but very embarrassing for him and the school. Dr. Henriksonn and his wife, both in their 70's, were seen by some neighbors sunbathing on the deck in their own backyard—in the nude.

Apparently, the neighbors who reported them had just moved in and had some young kids and they didn't want their children to see the good Doctor and his wife in the buff. Trust me, no one wanted to see that.

The other two neighbors, who could see into the backyard, had always ignored Dr. Henriksonn and knew he was a little quirky. The new neighbors didn't ignore it. It made quite a scene at the university and Dr. Henriksonn retired rather than take the suspension they were offering. So, that incident, rightly or wrongly, influenced me not to take any other religion courses. In retrospect...my loss.

My system of just paying attention in class and not studying very much worked well for me. That is, until one day on a History exam when I looked at the test questions and realized that I didn't recognize hardly anything on the exam. I had not done any of the required reading or studying. I just figured I would get by, like I had in the other classes. Sometimes, being smart was an advantage in that you didn't have to work as hard. Sometimes it got you in trouble—like now.

I looked at all the questions on this end of term exam and only knew about 25% of the answers—I was in big trouble. By taking short cuts and not studying and doing the work I had put myself in a deep hole. I did not know what I was going to do, when suddenly, opportunity again presented itself to me on a golden platter. The professor stood up and told us he is going down the hallway to his office and we are to bring him our exams when we finish them.

Wow!

As soon as he left our classroom, I got up from my desk, mentioned something about feeling sick to those around me and also walked out of the room. Only, I wasn't sick. I went to the next empty classroom, got out my history book and looked up all the answers to the questions I didn't know and completed the exam.

Guess what? I made 100 on the exam and enhanced my sterling reputation as one of the smartest guys around.

That professor should not have left us alone in the classroom. No way he should've done that. How could he trust a bunch of 18 and 19 year olds to be on their own? What a senseless act. I would've never done what I did if he didn't give me the opportunity. It was all his fault—at least, that was the excuse I used in my mind for the next 50 years. It was his fault I cheated. Right, George?

The only positive to come of that episode was that it scared me really good. From then on I worked a little harder to prepare for the exams. Not a lot harder, just a little harder. I didn't want to be faced with that situation again. I never cheated on tests or exams again, but I did start a new kind of cheating that was a lot more lucrative.

I met a guy who was a year ahead of me in school, but we had a few of the same classes together and we became very good friends. We liked the same things and chased a lot of the same girls. But with the girls, he was more successful than me...way more successful.

Richie had the gift of gab. He could walk up to any girl and start a conversation. He was never nervous or fumbling for words, he was just smooth. Sometimes, we would be sitting in the student union, drinking a Pepsi and watching the girls walk by. I'd comment on a particularly cute girl and Richie would say, "I could date her."

At first, I thought he was like all the rest of us...full of crap! He wasn't. Richie could walk up to a girl he'd never seen before, start a conversation and end up arranging a date for Saturday night with her. It was truly amazing and I was truly very jealous and envious of his ability and suaveness. I was still a hick. I distinctly remember two occasions when extremely attractive girls walked by and he made his comment that he could date them anytime he wanted to. The first time it happened, I called his bluff and bet him $10 he couldn't get a date with this girl. I lost the $10.

19

The second time it happened, the recently crowned Homecoming Queen came by with a group of her friends and I knew what he was going to say. Therefore, I beat him to the punch and said "Well, there's one girl you'll never date." He looked at me and said "How much?" I wanted to get my money back, so I said "Twenty bucks. And it'll be the easiest money I ever made." Let me ask you this, how many guys would ever walk up to a group of girls, a group of girls that he didn't know, mind you. Then pick out the prettiest girl in the bunch and start talking to her? Then, ask her for a date in front of the other girls? This was insane, but, this was Richie. You know how it ended, don't you?

Richie had a new car and seemed to always have plenty of money. Whereas I had a good supply of quarters, he had folding money, and lots of it. I figured his family was rich and he was just a spoiled rich kid, I was wrong.

He was from a neighboring town and both his parents worked in the local mill for probably not much more than minimum wage. Richie told me he had a job after school and on weekends as a deliveryman for a local appliance and furniture company. Okay, I still didn't quite understand how Richie had a new car and money and clothes all on a deliveryman's salary. It didn't make sense to me.

After many nights talking and many days spent building trust with each other, Richie let me in on his little secret. He was stealing appliances from the warehouse and selling them for cash. But, somehow,

Richie made it sound like it was okay what he was doing, that the company never really missed these items (they were over–stocked) and they didn't care anyway. And, there was a job opening working with him at this company and he recommended me to his boss. Goodbye Tom—hello Richie.

Richie figured out that the company he worked for had a very unstructured and uncaring way of storing their appliances in the warehouse outside of town. When delivery trucks from appliance manufacturers would deliver truck loads to the warehouse, Richie would sign for receiving the goods, then, slightly alter the number received. Maybe they delivered 37 window air conditioners one day; Richie would alter the 37 to look like a 33 and thus have 4 unaccounted for air conditioners.

He'd do the same for toasters; easy to alter 88 toasters to look like 80 toasters. Can openers, fans, mixers, drills, etc., etc., etc.– he was smuggling these "extra" items out in his delivery truck and selling them to friends and black market associates. The huge appliance manufacturers would never miss 2 or 3 fans. The store he worked for never knew about the "missing" items. They only knew about what Richie had signed for, and as far as he knew, they never inventoried their warehouse. He had quite a thriving business going and he needed help. This is where I entered the picture.

I never felt entirely comfortable with what we were doing. I knew in no uncertain terms that he was stealing and that it was wrong. But I helped him anyway. Richie had the ability to explain things in a way that made perfect sense, even though you knew it did not make sense. But, Richie was really the one stealing the goods, not me, right? It was easy money and it was easy selling the stuff. This is where Richie needed me to help him. He would make all the deals for the appliances, and I'd make the deliveries he couldn't make and bring the money back to Richie. Then, he'd give me a cut of the profits.

We'd take an air conditioner that may sell for $299 in the store and sell it on the street for $100. We sold fans for $25, drills for $20, on and on and on. Truthfully, every time I sold an item I was scared I was going to be caught—but it didn't stop me. I kept on doing it.

The money was a great incentive to ignore my morals and lower my integrity. Fortunately for me, Richie graduated from college and our little "business" ended at the end of the school year. I was both relieved of the tension of what I was doing and disappointed that I didn't have a steady income any longer. Sometimes, I wish I'd never met Richie and had never entered into this illicit venture. He sure led me down a slippery path. That darn Richie!

Richie ended up in his hometown and opened a jewelry store on Main Street. I visited him once after we'd both graduated and he gave me a tour of his store and took me out to lunch. We rode by his house, which seemed to me to be very expensive, and we had a nice conversation. Neither of us mentioned our past dalliances. Richie kept the conversation on his current business, how well he was doing, and made the point of telling me how he was engaged to the sexiest woman in town. They were planning a wedding the next spring. Richie never told me how much he loved this woman, or that he had found his "soulmate." He just kept describing how attractive she was and how all his buddies were jealous of him. I congratulated him on the engagement and the success of his business. We shook hands and promised to keep in touch. I think we both knew that would never happen.

———

I had saved enough of my ill-gotten money so that I didn't have to work my last year in college. That gave me more time to enjoy the company of some coeds I'd been noticing. One young lady in particular caught my attention, a junior with long dark hair and a beautiful smile. Emily was indeed a beauty and we started chatting with each other in the student union between classes, which soon led me to ask her on a date.

I wasn't like Richie. I had to talk to her a few times to build up courage and sort of get the feeling she wouldn't say no. Emily was from a small town near Washington, D.C. called Annandale; she liked going back home whenever she could. She came from a large family and had a lot of old girlfriends back home. At college is where Emily bloomed. She grew from skinny and plain in high school to shapely and gorgeous in college—at least in my eyes she did. I was smitten, and smitten hard.

She majored in Art History for some unknown reason. What in the world does someone do with a degree in Art History? Emily was the kind of girl you did not kiss on the first date, nor did you hold hands in the movies either. It took a good "getting to know you" period before any of that. But, I didn't mind, I just enjoyed being with her. Emily seemed more mature than her years—certainly more mature than any of the other girls I'd dated—and way beyond my maturity level. We had a grand time with each other and enjoyed many of the same things—going to movies, out to the lake, dancing at some local clubs. To be so conservative and old fashioned, Emily could shag with the best of them, and even do a little dirty dancing close to midnight.

After a month or two we decided we'd be exclusive with each other, which we had been anyway. It was just sort of official now. Everything was fun with Emily...everything. I thought about her so much that I tried my hand at poetry, with the presumption that my poems could express my feelings for Emily, without me really saying them out loud. I gave her a few of them and she gushed and made the biggest deal over them..."Oh George, I can't believe you wrote a poem just for me." And, "You've got to get these published, they're incredible." Yep, they were incredible alright. A few years ago I found my notebook from college containing the original versions of my poetry. My memory of these poems is nowhere near the reality of these poems. Emily must've really liked me a lot.

Emily, you are as sweet as the morning mist,
It makes me think of last we kissed.

Your smile can carry me through the day,
Till I see you again and say "Hey".

Really, George?

This was a great time for me. I was in "deep-like" with Emily. We enjoyed our times together and I looked forward to seeing her as much as possible. We were very close with each other, right up to the point of sex, which was the unwritten, yet clearly understood, demarcation line in those times. I gave Emily my class ring and she wore it as a necklace. We talked of all sorts of things, even the future. We never discussed marriage, but the "L" word did make it into our conversations occasionally.

I really thought this is as happy as a boy can be... until I was invited to a fraternity party one night when Emily was home visiting her parents. Then, I discovered a new kind of happiness. I found that girls at fraternity parties who were drinking and smoking were not there for the intellectual stimulation...no, not at all. They were not interested in holding hands or discussing social issues, but they were interested in doing some dirty dancing. With the emphasis on "dirty".

I guess because I had a little money and a fairly new used car that I was targeted by some of these party girls. I became an easy conquest. Blondes, brunettes, even red- headed girls were all treated evenly and fairly by me. The only one who wasn't, was Emily. On weekends, I started lying to her saying that I needed to go home and study about 10:00 on

Saturday night and she believed me. Heck, the frat parties were just beginning to get going at 10:00; they usually lasted till about 3 or 4:00 AM. I could have my sweet Emily and have my not-so-sweet party girls all at the same time.

Why couldn't Emily have checked on me better? How could she believe my lies so easily? Why was she so naïve? Why was I so stupid? Well, the answer to that is when you're young and basically inexperienced with girls, it's hard to say no when opportunities are thrust upon you. Remember, this was 1961 or 62 maybe, the sexual revolution of the late 60's had not evolved yet. Sexual encounters outside marriage were deeply frowned upon and never discussed, yet they were in the dreams of every college boy I knew. And most likely every coed as well, who was prim and proper, wore her skirt below the knees, and danced to Lawrence Welk— but dreamed of twisting to Chubby Checker.

This "experimental period" as I refer to it, lasted a couple of months. I would go to at least one frat party each week, sometimes two. I still saw Emily on a very regular basis, but I rationalized in my warped little mind that going to these parties and indulging in sexual promiscuity was okay for guys to do, in fact, in was somewhat expected. You really needed to get this out of your system before marriage. I almost convinced myself that Emily wouldn't really mind. Sex can absolutely warp your sense of reality.

Everything continued on this little crooked road of mine just fine until Emily had a class seminar with one of the "party girls" from the fraternity socials. They were talking during a break in the class one day and of course, boys became a subject of conversation. The girl Emily was talking to was named Gilda. I always remembered her because years later one of the stars of "Saturday Night Live" was named Gilda. Every time I watched that show, I was reminded of those lurid nights at the frat parties.

Emily and Gilda began talking and soon Gilda began detailing tales of love and romance with a guy she just met, George. He was so wonderful, so caring and just loved having fun. Then she started telling Emily, very graphically, all the things he was doing with her in private and promising to do with her in the future. I learned that at these frat parties, girls love to be lied to, and the bigger lie you tell them, the more they believe it. And that big lies equal even bigger carnal advantages. Emily, being sweet and innocent, was interested in Gilda's lurid details of romantic conquests, until she heard George's last name. Which happened to be her George's last name, and my last name.

Emily never forgave me for those transgressions. As hard as I tried to win her back, as much as I told her Gilda meant nothing to me, she was gone. Everything happens for a reason. Sometimes the reason is that you are stupid and make bad decisions. I was sad over the way things ended—I was sorry that she caught me. I was not sorry for all the good times I had partying with Gilda (and others).

There's a big difference there.

Several years after college, I ran into Emily on a cruise ship, of all places.

It was a large ship with about 5,000 passengers and we didn't run into each until the last day on board. She was stunningly beautiful and I was at a loss for words when we faced each other. She was with a tall, skinny guy, with a bad haircut and a thin mustache. I was with—well, I was with someone I shouldn't have been with. We looked in each other's eyes for about five seconds, did not speak, then walked away. Those five seconds lived in my brain for about five more years.

———————

During these college years I remember only doing one other thing which I'm not proud of. I'm sure there were others, but it was long ago and my memory fades. I was at one of the frat parties one night and went to the restroom and someone had left a bag of marijuana on the toilet tank top. I didn't smoke marijuana, I thought it was a big waste of money. About the only thing I indulged in was a beer or two.

Looking back at that period, I was probably a bit boring—if you discount the stealing and cheating part. Instead of leaving the marijuana where it was, or minding my own business—I put it in my coat and left with it. The next day I sold it for $20. I did not feel bad about this theft. It was an illegal drug and shouldn't have been there. Whoever brought it to the party could have been arrested. I was really saving them from getting in trouble. True, I shouldn't have stolen it. But I did do a good deed, didn't I?

The only person I didn't try to take advantage of or use during my college years was my mom—she was my mom and I loved her. Mothers seem to have the ability to love their kids regardless of the circumstances, regardless of their shortcomings, regardless of their deeds and words and actions. (I'm hoping Jesus will have a lot of these same qualities when I meet him soon). My mom was a good athlete when she was in school and kept very active throughout her life. She swam, she ran, she played tennis and even golfed for a bit. But, golf was a little too time-consuming for her. She had a husband and three boys to take care of.

Since I was the oldest, my mom kept trying to get me to do things with her: shoot some baskets in our backyard goal, go swimming with her, play tennis with her—but sports just didn't interest me. Even though I know I was the favorite (the oldest usually are), she was really happy when my youngest brother developed a love of sports, now she had someone to play with. Teddy was an athlete. He was good at everything and he and mom had some good battles on the tennis courts. I still remember the first day Teddy ever won a match from mom. He was so proud of himself, you'd have thought he won Wimbledon. And I could tell mom was even prouder...she lost the match, but she was seeing her son grow and prosper. That's the way mothers are.

I also loved my dad, but I used his generosity to my advantage. My dad worked hard to provide for his family, feeding and educating three boys was not a simple task. However, I don't ever remember asking my dad for anything that I truly needed, that he didn't get for me or my brothers. Now, he didn't buy us a pony, or go-carts, things like that, but we never lacked for anything else. He was a great dad and I loved him.

If we messed up, he would whip us (he'd probably go to jail for that today), but it only showed that he loved us and wanted us to truly learn "right from wrong". The whippings didn't happen often and were more symbolic, since he really didn't use much force. It hurt a lot worse if we did something wrong and instead of a whipping, Dad told us he was "disappointed" in us. I'd much rather have a whipping than to hear my Dad say he was disappointed in me. A whipping only lasts for a minute or two, disappointment lasts a lifetime.

Dad knew I was working in college, but he had no idea I was making all this "dirty" money. He thought I was the typical broke college student. Whenever I came home from school, he always asked me if I needed any money. I would always say "No dad, I'm okay" knowing that he would give me $40 or $50 anyway, and I kept taking his money. Was that wrong? In retrospect, I guess it was. I didn't need his money; I was fine, just selfish I guess. But aren't dads supposed to help their sons out financially? Isn't that part of their responsibility? "But, what about your responsibility as a son, George?" That little voice in the back of my mind is not so little any longer.

I graduated with a good GPA and a degree in Business Administration from Virginia Commonwealth University. I had a solid resume and a good work history, and had a choice of several jobs when I left school. Unfortunately for me, I chose the highest paying job, instead of taking a job I might actually enjoy. Some recruiters came to our campus and asked several graduating seniors from the business department to interview with their respective companies. This would be my first formal interview so I wanted to look sharp Friday morning when I went there. At the time I only had one suit and I hadn't worn it since Uncle Ed's funeral last year. I checked it out Thursday and it seemed in bad shape, wrinkled and sloppy.

I looked in the yellow pages and found a cleaner across town named "One Hour Cleaners." I grabbed my suit, jumped in the car and took off. There was a very friendly Asian man at the counter. As I walked in, I showed him my suit and he said, "Don't worry. I'll have it looking brand new for you." Great news! I said. "Thanks. I'll be back in a couple of hours to pick it up." "What?" he said, "It won't be ready till Monday." I was confused and looked back at him and said, "Monday?

31

Your sign says 'One Hour Cleaners.' He replied, "Oh, that's just the name of the company. We can't actually do that."

So, I wore a hand-me-down from dad, and it worked just fine.

From the very start, I hated my job and despised going in to work every day. I think my boss knew I was smarter than him. I was definitely more educated than he was. And, he probably figured I would eventually pass by him in the promotion game. He didn't like me and I had little respect for him. He was someone who supervised his staff through intimidation and bullying. These were the days before "political correctness" was in vogue and he could say virtually anything to anybody without repercussions in those times.

I'll always remember my boss there. His name was Harold Crean—I always called him "cretin" behind his back, and soon everyone was referring to him as the "cretin." He had the habit of calling any black person a nigger (excuse my language), and he used this disgusting term with all our minorities—except one. L.J. was big—I mean BIG. Harold was an idiot, but he wasn't stupid. He pretty much left L.J. alone, except for referring to him as "boy" every once in a while.

Harold didn't actually molest any of the women working for him. Not blatantly anyway. However, he would always be staring at their breasts a little too long, or stand a little too close to them when ordering them around. Little things that were just this side of creepy. He seemed to know his job, but with only a high school education, I'm also sure he was, not so much intimidated by me, as concerned that I was there to take his job away from him. So, he treated me like crap. He called me "college boy", "pretty boy" or any other name he thought would denigrate me to the rest of the staff. Heck, I liked being called "pretty boy"; it reinforced my already lofty opinion of myself.

If we had to work overtime, Harold would never tell us until about 10 minutes before it was time to go home, and then snicker as he walked away. If anyone ever made a mistake (and we all did), he would verbally abuse that person so badly that most of the females ended up in tears and most guys simply wanted to beat the tar out of him. But, you couldn't, jobs were too valuable. But, oh, how we all wished that one day L.J. would snap and give old Harold what he had coming to him. But, L.J. always kept his cool. Of course Harold was never foolish enough to abuse him like he did the rest of us.

He loved being able to bully and humiliate the "college boy," and as much as I tried to act as though it didn't bother me. It did. It really did. When a job was posted on the bulletin board for an opening in the shipping department, I quickly applied and after a perfunctory interview, was hired for the job. Old Harold the cretin didn't have me to kick around anymore, I left his department without so much as a "goodbye".

Now Harold could continue the domination and subjugation of his staff in relative peace and quiet, without the fear that some "pretty boy" was going to take his job. Years later I heard that old Harold, a life-long bachelor, had married a mail order bride from the Philippines. That was quite a surprise, given his penchant for discriminatory comments about any non-white person. I guess it proves love conquers all; or, that you never truly know what's inside a person.

Our company made nuts and bolts and small fixtures for the automotive industry. Our largest customers were Ford, General Motors, Chrysler and the newly emerging Japanese manufacturers. One of my responsibilities in this new job was to keep accurate records of shipments and receipts and ensure the billings and payables were made on time. Actually, it was a simple job and any high school graduate could have done it.

I was bored with it within a month. I volunteered for other duties just to break the boredom, and was given the responsibility of negotiating with carriers over rates and schedules. This was fun, dealing with people and companies, trying to get the best deals and service available. It didn't take me long to figure out there was a lot of opportunities for corruption and a lot of "shady" characters in trucking and transportation.

The major automotive companies in the Detroit area were probably 90% of our business and it was extremely important that we keep them happy. It was quite obvious we could barely keep up with demand and routinely had to send our products for next day delivery, which was becoming very expensive. I was tasked with trying to cut this cost and find cheaper, yet reliable means to get our products from Virginia to

Detroit. I was in my element now and looking forward to this challenge.

Through negotiations with several different companies for next day freight service, I came to know a gentleman (and I use that term loosely) of Russian descent who had been in America about eight years. He started a local delivery company and kept branching out until he could now offer service throughout the eastern United States on a limited basis. He didn't have much overnight business. He was still mostly a local carrier. He wanted more. Nikita, or Nicky as we called him, was a very affable guy and spoke pretty good English until he became excited or upset. Then, you couldn't understand anything he was saying. It became a mixture of broken English, Russian and curse words—all molded together into something only his staff and shady set of drivers could understand.

Nicky told me he was actually from Latvia and didn't consider himself Russian—he was Latvian. But, he did serve in the Russian army and had killed a man before. I learned later that you really can't believe everything Nicky tells you. In fact, you'd be better off not believing anything Nicky told you. He told me he had four children, then another time, he said he only had three. How can you make that mistake? He walked with a slight limp, which he told me happened when he was shot while he was in the army. He told our forklift driver it happened in a car wreck, and told our foreman he was born with a club foot. This, in essence, was Nicky.

He wanted our business in the worst way. He kept making sales calls with me to try and get more business and ingratiate himself with me personally. He had a few local deliveries, but wanted the more lucrative, long distance routes as well. I enjoyed talking to him because you never knew what kind of wild stories he would come up with. Every weekend brought some wild, new adventure in the life of Nicky and he loved regaling me with his tales of conquest in the bedroom and the card room. If Nicky were to be believed, at least half the women in eastern Virginia had succumbed to his manliness. The other half were too ugly and he had to turn them away.

The car business was really booming, and it was all we could do to keep up with orders. Overnight deliveries from us to Detroit became a daily occurrence. Sometimes we used FedEx, or UPS or Airborne for the small packages, but often times we had several pallets that needed delivery to the auto giants in order for us to keep them happy, and thus, keep their business. This required a truck delivery from here in Virginia up to Detroit—flying several heavy pallets of nuts and bolts was simply too cost prohibitive.

I started taking bids on this overnight delivery route from several local and regional carriers. It was very competitive and all the companies were reasonably close to each other with their final bids— except for one. Guess who that one was? Our good friend Nicky had undercut his competitors by a substantial amount. At first, I thought he'd made a mistake in his calculations and called him in to make sure he knew what he was submitting. Oh, he knew alright. He knew exactly what he was doing. Nicky was smart, conniving and quite a bit on the shady side—apparently, I had met my Russian soul mate.

———————

Whereas all the conventional companies like FedEx and UPS paid their drivers normal set wages—Nicky did not. He had an underground pipeline of Russian refugees, recently immigrated into our country, some legally—some not. All of these refugees had very little money, were unable to speak the language, and had no relatives or friends to help them with anything. Well, this is where Nicky came in. He would hire these broke, desperate people to drive his trucks and then pay them slave wages (which they thought were great.) They actually thought Nicky was doing them a favor.

Therefore, Nicky could undercut the competition by slashing the salaries he paid to drivers and be the lowest bidder on all new business.

When I finally understood how Nicky was operating and what he was doing, I quickly saw opportunity knocking at my door. I presented my offer to Nicky (knowing he had no alternative, other than accept it) and suddenly he and I became partners in collusion. Here's how things worked at the time. The going rate for a truck to drive to Detroit was $1500, which was the lowest bid, before Nicky entered the picture.

Here's how the new deal would work: I would award the contract to Nicky's company for $1350 (which was saving our company $150 per load), I then became a hero to our financial guys. Nicky was then making an extra $350 on each load, of which he paid me $150 per load, as my fee for him getting the business. So, the company was making $150 per load, I was making $150 per load and Nicky was making $200 per load—win-win-win.

At the time, we were shipping a load to Detroit every day, sometimes six days a week. I was making $750-$900 most weeks TAX FREE! And who was I hurting? The company saved money because they got the lowest bid. Nicky made money. I made money. The drivers had plenty of work, so everybody won...except my conscience. Deep down, I knew this wasn't right, but when Nicky would give me $750 a week, in cash, I sort of turned the other cheek—so to speak. I found a way to rationalize it and quiet the little voice in the back of my mind.

He could've turned my offer down. He could've upped his bid, he could've done a lot of things...but he didn't. He was a greedy, conniving man who took advantage of immigrants and let money be the base of his judgments. Why couldn't he just be up front and honest? It's very disappointing to know there are people like Nicky out there, taking advantage of people every day, in every situation. I was very disappointed in him...and me.

There was a secretary working at our company who was a few years older than me and she was a very attractive "older lady".

When I was 25 or so, she was 30, almost too old to look at. I really never spoke to her except to say "Good morning" or "How are you today?" Julie didn't go to college, but she did take the entrance exam to beauty school, and decided it wasn't for her. She listened to soft rock music on her radio. She read The National Enquirer at lunch. She painted her fingernails a different wild color each week, and she was very, very married. We had nothing whatsoever in common. Except, I liked the way her short skirts fit her.

I found out later she would intentionally walk near me in the break room, with her short skirts, and sway her hips provocatively when I was around. She knew what she was doing...she knew exactly what she was doing. I was single, young and hormonally excited and saw nothing wrong with this All American activity—girl watching.

Over a period of months we began speaking more often, then, we might have a Coke break together.

Occasionally we'd have a short lunch in the break room. I'd listen to her complain about her sorry, good-for-nothing husband who didn't "understand" her. She started sending me little notes, like "That color looks really good on you today." Or, "I like your new haircut." Simple little inconsequential musings, except for the fact that each little note I received elevated the level of my hormonal anxiety that was already nearly bursting.

Soon, the lunches and breaks with Julie were the highlights of my day. I looked forward to those little meetings more than anything. We began sitting a little too close to each other at breaks, not overtly, just enough that our elbows sometimes touched each other—by accident of course. Sometimes, my knee might brush against hers as I sat down, and I'd never smelled a woman who smelled as good as Julie did. Whatever it was she was wearing, it was working.

It's hard to imagine now, but these were the days before computers were commonplace in the office (or at home). The company had one large computer, but desktops were still a thing of the future. So, handwritten notes and phone calls were the basic forms of communication. Our note-writing started taking on bolder and bolder sexual innuendos. I was really enjoying this game.

One day Julie told me she and a girlfriend of hers were going shopping Saturday at a place near my apartment and asked if I was going to be home that afternoon. I hadn't thought about it, but, yes I'd be there. She said they might drop by to see me. Wow!

That was unusual—I wondered about this girlfriend of hers. I sat around Saturday afternoon wishing the clock would PLEASE move a little faster, then I saw Julie's car drive into the lot. She got out...alone.

Where was her friend?

Well, as you can probably guess, one thing led to another, which led to another and before you can spell fornication, we were deep in the act. Did it bother me that I was messing around with a married woman? Obviously not enough. Heck, I wasn't married and all I could see (with those sexual blinders on) was the fun and excitement in it. Julie was the one who initiated it all, she wrote all the notes.

She made the phone calls. She could have stopped it anytime. All she had to do was say "No, I can't do this, I'm a married woman." But she never did. And neither did I.

We kept this up for several months, meeting after work, on weekends, here and there. It was quite the adventure I thought. Sounds rather immature on my part now, but back then, I was thinking it was all just one, big adventure. Two or three hours in a flop house hotel, back in the woods of a local park, in my car parked out at the lake. It was all fun and games on my part; nothing serious whatsoever, nothing meaningful, nothing lasting.

The entire time I was messing around with Julie, I was also looking for a "nice" girl to date; but didn't seem to find one. I probably wasn't looking all that hard. Julie was fun and she was very sexy, but I knew that what we had was ONLY fun, I knew it would never last, that it was just a temporary, sexual manifestation of my fledgling manhood (or my stupidity, which were both the same I imagine).

It was clear Julie and her husband were not close. To hear her side of the story, the whole marriage was a mistake and she regretted every single day of it. He spent all his time hunting or fishing, or playing with guns with his buddies and never did anything with her—not that she would want to anyway. They got married soon after high school, when sex was more important to him than hunting raccoons and possums. According to Julie, soon after marriage, the raccoons, possums, rabbits and deer soon garnered all his attention and she was left in a loveless, lonely marriage.

I didn't really enjoy hearing all this stuff about her husband (especially the guns part), I preferred to ignore him and the marriage thing and just think of Julie as fun and excitement. It was much easier that way. So, we continued our charade over the months. It was really easy for me, I didn't have to take her out to dinner or to a movie—just use her for the "fun" stuff.

Then one fine day Julie tells me her husband is going on his two- week National Guard duty and that she wants us to "Go away" for a few days. What exactly did she mean by this "Going away"?

Apparently, she had been planning this adventure for a few weeks, knowing that her husband would be camping out in the wilds of north Georgia with his Guard unit. She found a five day cruise she wanted us to go on together, so we could really get to know each other. Huh? Truly, I knew her as well as I wanted to know her. But, it's hard saying no when you're young and in deep lust.

I'd never been on a cruise before. I found out quickly that you get to know someone really well in the cabin of a cruise ship. Two people stuffed inside a compartment about 8' by 12', with a bathroom barely large enough to turn around in. Without going into a lot of detail, suffice it to say there are very few secrets when you're sharing a cabin with someone on a cruise ship. Two days into the five day cruise and I was ready to go home.

Spending 24 hours a day with someone was quite different than spending a couple of hours in a hotel room—which is all we'd ever done before. She thought everything was fantastic and seemed to be having the time of her life, whereas, I was feeling cramped, penned in, suffocated and a bit guilty. That darned voice in the back of my mind didn't seem to enjoy cruise ships either.

Every meal with Julie, laying out by the pool with Julie, going to shows with Julie, dancing with Julie, shopping with Julie——truly, I was Julie'd out! The happier she became, the more miserable I became. The only good time I had the last three days of that cruise was when I went scuba diving by myself, only because she wasn't certified. I can't describe the peace I felt under the water. There was no Julie around, just me and the yellow, blue and red fish of the Caribbean.

If it were possible, I'm sure I would've swum back to the U.S. that day. Just so I wouldn't have to endure the rest of the cruise. But I didn't. Instead, I swam back to the boat when they signaled us in. I went back on the cruise ship and politely smiled. Then made my way to the nearest bar on deck and ordered two shots of the strongest drink they had... and I'd never had shots before!

We did all the things you're supposed to do on a cruise to have fun: we went to the midnight buffet every evening, we laid by the pool and had big, tall drinks with fruit and little umbrellas in them (she saved all her umbrellas). We visited the hot tub and the spa, played bingo and ate ice cream anytime we wanted to. Oh, what fun!

Except, I wasn't having fun. It's very hard to PRETEND to have fun when you're actually miserable.

Somehow, I made it through to Friday, the last day of the cruise. Finally this torture was going to end— that's when I saw Emily. She was getting off one of the ship's elevators as we were getting on. Time stopped. The earth quit revolving, and the galaxy ceased existing. It's amazing how long five seconds can last. Emily looked at me and didn't blink or speak. But her eyes never left mine. I was transfixed, unable to comprehend what was happening. Until Julie tugged at my arm and said, "Let's go! I want some ice cream."

How in the world did I ever let this woman talk me into doing this?

How could I let her use me like this? How was I going to get out of this? How I missed my sweet Emily... I really don't like cruising.

Well, Julie packed our luggage, tipped all the waiters and staff and said goodbye to our little sardine can of a room. Julie seemed a little emotional to be leaving. I was trying to hold back tears of joy. We finally made it to my car and started home. She was singing songs and making jokes; I was depressed, solemn and fervently trying to figure out how to exit this relationship gracefully.

Unfortunately, I found out quickly there is no way to exit an illicit relationship gracefully.

Somehow, Julie thought we had a future together. Honestly, I NEVER, ever hinted at any future, never discussed anything with her more than where we would meet next. I have no idea where she came up with this scenario. Love was never a subject of our conversations. When I told her I thought it would be best if we "cooled" it for awhile, she was not happy. I think she was looking at me as a way out of an unhappy marriage and as someone to lead her to the promised land.

She tortured me, threatened me and harassed me for weeks on end. She even went so far as to tell my boss that I was making sexual advances to her, and that she may even file a harassment suit against me and the company. This woman went from sweet and sexy to venomous and hateful before I knew what was happening.

College girls weren't like this when I broke up with them. I really liked college girls. Lesson learned...I would never mess around again with a married woman, no sir! There were certainly enough single girls out there who were gullible enough to fall for my cheating, conniving ways. As an end note to this sorrowful affair, Julie soon took up with an older man, left her pitiful husband and quickly became pregnant with twins. I hope they're happy.

Let me fast forward to the present day for a few moments. I've had to buy a recorder and tape my thoughts as I'm no longer able to type for any length of time. I found a young college girl to type all this stuff up and not charge me too much. If I were younger, or not sick, it might embarrass me to let a young lady read about my sordid past. It's still a bit weird for me to let someone else in on a lifetime full of secrets. But she has never flinched, never asked a question, never snickered, nor passed judgment (that I'm aware of).

I give her the tapes, she types them up and I pay her—and no, I don't even try to cheat her. It's hard for me now to stay awake for more than an hour or so at a time. I keep falling asleep, whether I want to or not. I fall asleep watching TV, eating soup and checking the computer. I even fell asleep on the toilet last week— that's a sad state of affairs, falling asleep on a toilet.

One of my goals is to be able to die here at my home. Not in some antiseptic hospital room, surrounded by overworked nurses, pooping in a pan, eating rubber chicken, or whatever else they think is "good" for me. They send a hospice nurse to my home every other day now to make sure I'm okay and don't need anything.

Unfortunately, it seems to be a different nurse each week and I have to keep explaining to them why I'm alone and don't have anyone I can call or rely on. It's bad enough I'm dying. Now I have to be humiliated by these total strangers each week, reminding me of my sorrowful plight.

The bad part of this whole illness, sickness and dying thing is that for some reason my mind is always fully alert and my memory is, if anything, enhanced. I guess it wouldn't be too awfully bad if I couldn't remember anything, or didn't know who I was, or what I'd done. But to be able to remember EVERYTHING is the topping I didn't want on this ill-tasting piece of cake. Oh, how I'd love to be strapped to a wheelchair, drooling all over myself, peeing in a tube, unable to even remember what my name was. Instead, here I am reliving all my deeds and regrets and feeling sorry for my broken body, spirit and heart. I am unable to forgive myself, unable to forget, unable to mend my broken heart and especially unable to mend the one heart I never wanted to break.

———

After the Julie debacle, and a few weeks of solitude and reflection, I met and started seeing a very successful single, young lady who was a financial planner. Dana was educated, very attractive, very sociable, very rich, and dumb as a dog's foot. Not intellectually, just in a common sense sort of way. She could negotiate to buy a new car, get the best financing available, then, forget to put gas in it until she ran out. And she never changed the oil in her cars or had them serviced— said she never thought about it. She knew everything there was to know about financial planning. She knew how stocks and mutual funds worked, the best investment schemes and how to make your money grow. She just didn't know very much about anything else.

Dana came from a wealthy family in Rhode Island and was a graduate of Notre Dame, which she was very proud of. She never let an opportunity pass without letting everyone around her know that she was Fighting Irish, through and through.

She was the type of fan who knew if her beloved Irish had won the game that day, but couldn't tell you who they played or the names of any players or coaches—the college equivalent of a Dallas Cowboys fan. Sorry about that, but us Redskins fans love to stick it to the Cowboys every chance we get.

Dana knew which Fortune 500 companies to invest in, which mutual funds were no-load opportunities and which weren't, and which was the best vacation spot: the Hamptons or West Palm Beach. But, she couldn't tell you which countries the United States fought in WWII, or if John McEnroe was a country music star, movie star or member of the Rolling Stones. To be so smart, she was clueless. At first I thought it was an amusing trait of hers, but later it bothered me that she could be so unaware of life, history and her surroundings. Then, I saw advantages in it. Why does my mind always work this way? Why am I always looking for ways to benefit myself, instead of trying to help others? Am I the only sneaking, deceitful, scoundrel out there?

Dana's job paid her a very nice salary. Her father made sure a lot of his friends and associates used Dana for their financial needs. She was set. She did not need the trust fund her father and grandfather had set aside for her—$100,000 from her grandfather and $500,000 from her dad. In addition, each Christmas, Dana told me her father gave her a check for $50,000, plus a check for $10,000 on her birthday. She had always invested this money and by now she could probably retire if she wanted to. Her condo was paid for, as were her car and any other debts us normal people might have had. It's nice being born into wealth.

I can't begin to list all the ways I took advantage of Dana without her ever knowing anything was happening. I'm not sure if I did this because I subconsciously resented Dana's wealth, or because it was just so darned easy. We both loved to travel, but she was so naïve about things. She was relieved when I would take care of all the arrangements, book the hotels and make the plane reservations, all she had to do was basically just show up.

We loved going to relaxing places like Miami, or Cozumel, or Phoenix. Places we could find a nice resort, lie around in the sun, have some drinks, eat well, just relax and enjoy things. I would make all reservations and pay for everything on my credit card and Dana would simply write me a check for half of the expenses. Only she never really knew what the expenses actually were.

The first time I did anything was simply for convenience. We stayed at a resort and the total bill for the weekend (room, meals and drinks) was $573. She asked me how much she owed me and instead of trying to somehow calculate half of $573, I just said "$300 will take care of it." Then, I started fudging even more. If our airplane tickets were $400 each, I would tell her they were $500 each. If the resort room rates were $125 a night, I'd tell her they were $150 a night.

Everything I paid for was inflated like this and she never questioned any of it. There were some vacations we took where I actually made money on the trip! Was this wrong? Undoubtedly, yes. I knew it then, I know it now, but money meant virtually nothing to Dana. It was just a means to keep score with and something to accumulate.

Dana was gorgeous and very fun to be with, but her lack of knowledge of common sense things began to irritate me more and more. Unless it was something financial, I could tell her virtually anything and she'd believe me. We were in the car one day at a stop light, and the car in front of us was from North Carolina. Dana looked at the license plate on the car and said "First in Flight...what does that mean?"

Now, I thought everyone in the country knew that "First in Flight" refers to the Wright Brothers first flight at Kill Devil Hills on the coast of North Carolina.

Obviously, Rhode Islanders thought a couple of mechanics from Ohio flying some contraption on a beach in North Carolina was not worthy of their attention. So, me being me, I said "That means North Carolina was the first state to take "Flight" from the union at the beginning of the Civil War." "Oh", she said, "that makes sense", and she continued reading the Wall Street Journal.

Several weeks later I convinced her the South had actually won the Civil War, but had only ceded victory to the North in order to sustain the union for financial purposes. And, since it involved something financial, she believed it!

The more gullible I found her, the more cruel I became in the things I told her. I found it totally amazing that an adult human being, a graduate of a major university, a successful business woman could actually believe that on NASA's first flight to the moon, they wanted Neil Armstrong to fly around Mars first. To presumably take pictures for possible landing sites on later missions, before he actually landed on the moon. I told her the Spanish/American War was fought to protect our orange groves in Florida from the Cubans and Mexicans who were trying to steal the fruit. I know...I was cruel. But was it my fault she was so dumb?

The final straw for me happened as we were lying on a blanket at Virginia Beach discussing places we'd like to visit and things we'd like to do. I told her I'd like to visit Alaska and see that vast country which seemed so immense and beautiful. She looked at me with those gorgeous blue eyes and said, "I think my passport has expired, I'll have to check it." I looked at her and said, "Passport?" "Yes," she said, "I think it's expired." Trying to control myself, not wanting to say anything mean or demeaning that would ruin the rest of the trip, I simply said, "Okay, check it when we get back home." I knew I could not continue very much longer with Dana if I was to keep my sanity.

Her intoxicating beauty could not overcome her lack of intellectual diversity. When we finally had the conversation where I told her our relationship was not working for me and that we should both move on. Instead of crying or asking why, or getting mad at me, she simply looked at me and asked if she owed me any money. Incredibly, I said no. I'd already taken advantage of her enough. No Dana... go grow your portfolio, invest in NASDAQ, diversify your assets...but every once in a while, please read something (anything) besides the financial section of the newspaper.

54

Sometimes, it's fulfilling and rewarding to simply sit and converse with a woman in a meaningful and engaging way. Of course, it does help if that woman is attractive and sexy. Maybe I'm being too picky, looking for the unattainable, searching for the lost treasure that's never meant to be found. Apparently, this period in my younger life, before marriage, was going to be an extended period of flirtations and less than meaningful relationships.

At the time, I was quite content to meet a young lady or two, have some fun and move onto other young ladies. After Dana, I didn't have any relationships lasting more than a few weeks or so. Eventually, I did meet a very intelligent woman, a college professor in fact. She was a joy to be around, had a great sense of humor and was stimulating to talk to, but, she just wasn't that pretty.

I was at some stuffy party one night where the main topic of conversation seemed to be whether chardonnay, zinfandel or pinot gris was the correct wine to serve with grilled salmon. I thought my head was going to pop from listening to this inane discussion. Then a woman walked up behind me, tapped me on the shoulder and asked if I wanted a Pabst Blue Ribbon. She said I looked to be a bit bored with the current conversation...ya think? I figured this average looking woman must be a working stiff like me to be drinking PBR, so off we went to the refrigerator and sure enough, there was six pack of Pabst just sitting there.

She handed me one. She took one and we popped the tops and took a good slug—first to quinch our thirst, second to wash away all the hogwash we'd been listening to. She then told me an amusing, off-color joke. I was really beginning to like this woman, she was fun. We talked the rest of the night, poked fun at most everyone else there and finished off the PBR. Good thing there was only one six- pack in the fridge— I'm not much of a drinker.

Janet was very nice, and certainly not ugly, but she also wasn't what you would describe as pretty. I wanted to be physically attracted to her, I tried to be, but I wasn't. Much like a good red wine, her wit was dry and perplexing. She was so much fun to talk to that I could almost convince myself that she was attractive and that she had an inner beauty— whatever that is. She may have had the sexiest voice I've ever heard. I loved talking to her on the telephone.

Our phone conversations would leave me in a state of near exhaustion, dreaming of that silky voice, just thinking of the possibilities. But, it never lasted. We'd go out for dinner and I'd find myself checking out other women, wishing I was with them, instead of Janet. I often wished I could've put Janet's brain inside Dana's body. What a combination that would have been. If only I had been close personal friends with Dr. Frankenstein.

Janet taught Philosophy at the University of Richmond and was in the final stages of finishing the dissertation which would complete her doctorate work. I could discuss nearly any subject with Janet and she could give and take ideas and opinions as well anyone I'd ever been around. "George, is physical beauty that important to you? Aren't companionship and intellectual stimulation just as important?" Ummm...no; sorry, but it's just not. I'm sorry, I wanted it to be, I tried to convince myself that I was physically attracted to Janet. At times, I thought I could be. She was so much fun to be around that I couldn't just end things, so, I didn't.

I dated Janet off and on (way more off than on) for about 18 months, but never steadily. Sadly, I only seemed to call her when I was in between other girls and needed some companionship and fun. I knew whenever I called her, she would always be available. We'd have some fun, enjoy each other's company; then I would meet someone else and ignore old Janet until I needed her again. I was only thinking of me–surprise! I never knew if Janet saw other men or not. I really never thought about it. I was too absorbed in myself and my own needs to think about her...or anyone else for that matter.

I'm quite certain Janet wanted more from me than I was willing to give. She even asked me one night if I thought we had a future. Rather than ruining the moment, I deflected the question with something humorous and quickly changed the subject. I'm sorry to admit this, but I used Janet and her companionship, friendship and other things for my own pleasure and needs—with little thought of hers. I never misled Janet, never hinted there would be anything more serious or lasting. She knew I dated other women, but she didn't seem to mind. Sometimes I wonder about that. Finally, on one of my sabbaticals from her friendship, she met someone nice and got married.

I didn't know any of this until I called her one Saturday night when I had nothing else to do, after a couple of months of ignoring her. Her husband answered the phone. I thought that was odd, a man answering Janet's phone, but he put her on and after a minute or two of "How are you's?" she told me she was married. She had known Charles for several years and that she finally decided now was the right time to accept his offer of marriage.

Apparently, Charles had been courting her since college and had asked her repeatedly to marry him. She didn't say so on the phone, but I had the feeling she wanted to say, "Since you were never going to ask me, I decided to take the best offer available." But, she didn't, she was better than that. She did tell me it would be a good idea not to call her again—and I never did.

Back at work, my little side ventures with Nicky had slowed considerably. Upper management had found a way to work our production schedules better so that all the overnight deliveries were mostly uncalled for any longer. I was sad to see that little business go away. So, I started looking for other higher paying jobs—I was used to the money and needed a bigger paycheck to keep up my lifestyle. When the daily deliveries to Detroit stopped, Nicky came to see me with an assistant. His assistant was beautiful (in a slutty sort of way), she had on heels that were a little too high, a dress that was a little too short, and cleavage that was a little too revealing. And, since she barely spoke English, I was almost certain she was not an administrative assistant at all.

Nicky was using his assistant as a lure for me to give him more business. This poor girl was being prostituted out by Nicky in hopes of gaining more money for him and his business. I hate to admit this, but if we'd had any business to give Nicky, his lure may have caught me. However, it was over. I hope the young lady somehow got away from Nicky, I never saw her again. Nicky, however, thrived over the years. He had billboards and commercials on television that made him seem like the American success story of the century.

Truth can be quite an illusion.

Almost immediately I found an opportunity I was interested in.

This small company in town was owned by an older husband and wife who lived in New Jersey. They wanted to stay up there more often because of their health concerns and their disdain for the bucolic lifestyle we apparently enjoyed in Virginia. They were looking for someone down here to run their small company. The office staff consisted of five women (all simple, plain and dumb), who were trying desperately to become pregnant. And it had a warehouse staff of eight guys of various ethnicities and ages.

They had a very nice thriving business. They'd buy products in bulk quantities and then ship units out individually, or sell locally, at huge mark-ups. They were making a fortune. I was hired as the plant manager, which basically meant making sure all deliveries and shipments were on time. Ensuring all bills were paid, payroll was met and simple office functions were taken care of. The girls did most of the work, and in fact, my job was pretty boring—which gave me too much time to think. A small part of our business was selling locally. This meant a lot of customers paid in cash, which I would deposit in the bank once or twice a week. You can see where this is leading can't you?

I didn't actually start skimming any money for at least a year, but the temptation was so overwhelming and the opportunity was so easy. I'm not going to lie to you and say I would have never taken any of this money. But I only started taking it when I thought the owners had lied to me and cheated me. When I was hired, I was told all employees received raises on June 1 of each year. Okay, that made perfect sense to me. I was hired on June 15, so I had to wait nearly a whole year to get a raise. I was okay with that.

So, June 1 of the next year comes and everyone gets their raise—except me. Thinking it was just an accounting oversight, I called them asked them to correct the oversight. Oh no, they said, you had to be employed with the company on June 1 in order to receive a raise, and since I wasn't hired until June 15, then I was not eligible for a raise.

I was the only salaried person on payroll. They could've paid me anytime, or given me a raise anytime. It had no bearing on the hourly people. I'd already grown their business more than they thought was possible, and this was how they were going to treat me? They were adamant I wait another year for a raise. Okay, I'd wait another year for a raise, but I wouldn't wait another day to start collecting some money. My average cash deposits in the bank would be around $800-1000 each week—nothing big; but large enough to cover $50 here or $75 there.

There was virtually no chance of this missing money ever being discovered. All cash deals of local sales were never accounted for in the master sales debit sheets. A lot of this money was kept in the office for minor expenses and petty cash transactions. Our main mailing and shipping business generated about a million and a half dollars of revenue, sometimes close to $2 million each year. Fifty or seventy-five dollars here and there would never be noticed.

I didn't need that money, but I felt cheated and as though they owed it to me. Plus, I had grown their business for them, increased their sales locally and nationally and stabilized the business so there were very few ups and downs in sales as there had been in the past. They were making more profits than ever before and they didn't have to come down here and deal with all these "hicks" as they thought we were. Just stay up there in the condo on the beach and we'll send you money each week—living the good life, while the rest of us did their work for them.

They shouldn't have denigrated everyone like they did. They could've elicited more loyalty with a little understanding and compassion instead of looking down their noses at their staff. But, it is what it is, and in my opinion, they got what they deserved. "But George, didn't you take their money?" Some could look at it that way, but they gave everyone small raises and never so much as a Christmas bonus, even for increasing their business beyond expectations. So, therefore, I was owed that money. Shut up!

The two owners would come down and visit the plant every 2-3 months. They'd stay overnight, usually on their way to Atlanta or Florida for a vacation. They always visited when it was time for yearly raises for the employees. They wanted to make a big show of giving their servants a $0.20 raise, while they were raking in hundreds of thousands of dollars in profits. I usually got a 2% raise, which they'd make a big fuss over.

They seldom said more than "Hello" to any staff members and seemed only to be concerned with how humid it was here. They insisted on taking me out to lunch when they visited. It was never a pleasant experience. The wife was a lush and upon being seated, immediately ordered a martini, followed by several other martinis.

Her husband usually had enough common sense to realize he was driving and limited himself to only a couple of drinks.

By the time lunch was over, she could barely stand up, let alone walk unaided. I don't know if it's because they drank so much or what, but I never once saw them leave a tip for any waitress or waiter ever. I would usually try to leave the table after they stumbled away and would discreetly slide a $5 or $10 bill behind for the poor staff people who had to endure the rude, demeaning way they treated everyone. Their food was never good enough. Their drinks weren't strong enough. The service was too slow. The temperature was either too hot or too cold. Nothing was ever good enough for the king and queen. It was torture being around them and the alcohol only made it worse. So, did I take some of their money? Yes. Did I feel bad about it? No.

9

During this time I met an extremely attractive woman at the YMCA. I started taking a swimming class there just to break the monotony of the day, and I thought it would help me lose some weight and stay in shape as well. I wasn't in bad shape, but my pants had begun to shrink around the waist and running was simply not my thing. I thought I could swim a few laps at lunch and help maintain my youthful appearance, while still eating and drinking anything I wanted to. I knew how to swim, but this class was for those who wanted to go to the next level and swim longer distances.

It was taught by a young man with 2% body fat who swam in college at William & Mary.

There were only six of us in the class. Me, a guy near my age with a huge pot belly, two older guys who were retired, a young overweight college-aged girl and a single young lady named Bea.

Bea was short for Belinda. I always thought Belinda was a better name than Bea, but Bea didn't like her given name. In fact, very few of her friends would know who you were referring to if you mentioned someone named "Belinda". What people would never forget though, was her beauty; to be more precise, her shape. Bea was gifted with a small waist, shapely hips, nicely proportioned legs and rather large breasts. The sight of Bea in a bathing suit stopped traffic.

I imagine if you asked ten guys to describe Bea's physical features, none of them would have remembered how her face was or what color her hair was, but they would never forget her body. For the record, she was very pretty with light brown hair. Bea had what every guy often dreamed of in a woman: a sexy body, a nice face, an alluring walk, a voice that would almost make you melt in your shoes and a fun and engaging personality. Yes, Bea was the type of girl whom guys were drooling over and dreamed of...until they met her three kids.

That first day when Bea walked out of the women's locker room into the pool area for our class, all activity stopped. I'm sure she was used to this type of behavior from men. We were not used to her.

The two older guys, who had been in the water, immediately started finger combing their hair, trying to re-establish the swooped over look they were now sporting. The young overweight girl blushed and the potbellied guy tried as hard as he could to suck in his gut. I was sure he would turn blue he held it so long. The instructor just ignored her, emphasizing what we already suspected—he was gay. I tried my best not to stare too much, while I also sucked in my stomach and tried to flex my meager chest muscles, while trying not to look like I was flexing. Bea made us all do these things. She couldn't help it.

Surprisingly, once we got in the water, I didn't think about Bea too much, I was more concerned with not drowning. Swimming laps in a pool is much more difficult than dog-paddling in the lake. I made one length of the pool okay, but could not make it all the way back. Fortunately, the part of the pool where I ran out of breath was only 5' deep and I could stand up. This was going to be harder than I thought it was. While I was panting, desperately trying to catch my breath, the young overweight girl passed me and looked as though she wasn't even breathing hard.

The two older guys seemed to have no problems either, but the potbellied guy didn't come close to completing first lap. The instructor had to throw him a float to hang onto so he wouldn't sink. Bea did okay, better than me, but it was clear we all needed a lot of practice and pointers if we were going to be lap swimmers.

We had the class three times each week, Tuesday, Thursday and Saturday at 12:00 noon. I think we all came on our lunch periods, except the two retired guys. By the third week, the potbellied guy quit, not even the sight of Bea in a bathing suit could keep him coming back. He must've really hated it. And honestly, if it hadn't been for Bea, I would have probably quit soon as well. This was much harder than I thought it would be. As you can surmise, week after week, conversations began to grow with Bea, one thing led to another, which led to coffee, then dinner, then a lot of stuff.

Bea was right up front and honest from the onset, she told about her three kids from the start. They were currently 8, 6 and 3 years old—one boy and two girls. After the youngest child was born, her husband simply walked in one day and told her he didn't love her anymore. In fact, he had never loved her. However, he had now found his "soul mate" and was moving to Chattanooga, Tennessee with her immediately. "No hard feelings", he said, and he would always financially support his children. What a prince!

Bea lived with her parents, so they could help take care of the kids. Swimming at lunch time was the only refuge she had from working and full-time motherhood. Bea had her first child when she was only nineteen years old, then the next one at twenty-one and the last one at twenty-four. Three kids when you're twenty-four years old—for me, that was unimaginable. I met her kids and parents...all nice and well mannered, but I was really only interested in Bea—and being with Bea. She couldn't go out often, but we did manage dinner and a movie a couple of times a week. Bea had been divorced now over two years and was a wonderful, caring, giving and beautiful person. It's truly hard to understand how a man could walk out on three children and a woman as wonderful as Bea.

Being with Bea was great. Even though she didn't have a college degree, she was well-read, professional and very intelligent. She'd only been on two dates since her divorce, one date only with two different guys. I didn't ask why she only dated each guy once. I guess Bea and I went out for 3-4 months. I just remember that it was all fun and she was one of the best women I'd ever known. I also knew I would never be able to adjust to, or commit to taking on the responsibility of three children. If Bea had been single, with no kids, I'm sure every guy in Virginia would have been chasing her. I know I would have. But three kids?

I knew in my heart I could never do that, as much as I wanted Bea, I knew I could never do that. I wanted to keep using her for my own personal pleasure, but I couldn't. Probably the only time I listened to the little voice in my head and did the right thing. I explained things to Bea. She understood, and that even made it worse. I felt like a complete heel. I thought a whole lot about calling Bea over the next few months. For one of the few times in my life, I did the right thing, and left that wonderful woman alone.

———

Work was going well and I was able to save quite a bit of money.

I bought a new car and some new clothes, but I really didn't have any other hobbies or outside interests to spend my time or money on. I dated around, but nothing long term, just something to do for fun. I didn't really like to travel by myself and I wasn't good at making friends. I didn't want to do anything with either of my brothers, because they would always expect me to pay for everything. So, I mostly kept to myself. This is when I first took up fishing.

I loved eating fish, but I never especially liked the idea of catching them or cleaning them. I wanted other people to do that. No, my idea of fishing was being alone on a lake, or by a river. Sometimes at the ocean, however, there were always too many people on a pier and I was more interested in being by myself than actual fishing anyway. I liked the idea of getting a small boat by myself, bringing a small cooler of soft drinks and sandwiches and rowing out to the end of lake, somewhere where no one else was. I didn't care if any fish were there or not. I was more interested in the solitude.

Most times, I never even baited my hook. You'd be surprised how many times I caught fish with no bait and not even trying. I knew Jesus made friends with fishermen. I was hoping He would be my friend somehow. I liked the idea of having a friend in Jesus. I liked everything I'd heard. I liked being able to talk to someone, to tell someone what I was thinking, what I liked and didn't like. I needed someone to confide in, someone to confess my deeds to. I wanted someone I could trust, who could help me quiet the little voice in the back of my mind. I wanted to be able to mold Jesus to fit my needs and desires; I basically wanted my own personal Jesus. I wanted Him to change for me. It took me a long time to understand that I'm the one who needed to change for Him.

So, I fished.

10

I only had one more fairly serious relationship. I guess you can classify being engaged as serious. It was way more serious for Elizabeth than it was for me.

I probably shouldn't have let it progress to the point of officially being engaged, but things just seemed to happen. Elizabeth was a true beauty, one year younger than me, with a good job as a real estate broker, which she was good at it. A born salesperson, she could make any house seem like the perfect fit for each potential buyer. She knew how to stage each house, present it with the utmost perfection and convince each customer that this house was made especially and uniquely for them. Elizabeth was also very ambitious.

We met at a pool party one summer and I couldn't help but notice a girl with great legs who always seemed to be at the center of each conversation. I began to join these conversations, not to hear what was being said, but to get a better look at those great legs and the woman they were attached to. Elizabeth and I seemed to hit it off. She laughed at all my jokes and seemed interested in everything I'd done. So, at the end of the party I asked her out and she accepted. That simple.

Elizabeth always wore the right clothes, always attended the socially acceptable functions, made sure she was always invited to the right weddings and the inner circle parties. She was a member of the Junior League, The Young Women's Auxiliary and the Daughters of the American Revolution. Seemingly, anyone could join any of these groups as long as you were female, well-connected and had money, or, the appearance of money. Elizabeth had the appearance of money.

She dressed well, had a new car, vacationed in all the right places, ate dinner at all the in vogue spots and was friends with all the right people. The only thing Elizabeth didn't have was money. It took all she made every week to keep living in the lifestyle she wanted to be accustomed to. She was looking for someone who first, could finance that lifestyle, and second, could impress her friends. I firmly believe love was a distant third on her priority list. Making the social scene and connections was immanently more important to Elizabeth than any personal feelings of love or commitment.

Of course, I didn't know any of this stuff initially. I was impressed with Elizabeth just as everyone else was. I was pretty happy she liked me and later seemed to be falling in love with me, but, there was always something I just couldn't identify with Elizabeth. That unknown something which just didn't add up. We obviously enjoyed our time with each other, but she enjoyed our times together more when we were seen by or doing something with people she wanted to impress. I found it a little odd that she would rather be at a social function with a bunch of blue-haired, moneyed debutantes, than alone with me. But, I went along for the ride.

Elizabeth usually got her way.

She always wanted us to do expensive things, go to the top end restaurants, take trips to fancy resorts. The more money it cost, the more she liked it. And, of course, she expected me to always pay for everything. She was from upstate New York and didn't mention her family much. Only that her dad worked hard to send her to Vassar, a very expensive and exclusive college for any prissy, debutante of the day. She made sure she wore her Vassar sweatshirts and tee shirts whenever she dressed down. She was not really impressed with my degree from Virginia Commonwealth University and never mentioned it around her friends.

Elizabeth only bought me one present that I remember. It was a Harvard sweatshirt that she said was on sale and would look good on me. What she really meant was that it would look good on her, standing next to a guy wearing a Harvard sweatshirt. I never wore it, not even to wash the car, or cut the grass in. I eventually gave it to my brother Frankie, who wore it all the time trying to impress the girls down at the local biker bar.

Elizabeth knew I was doing okay financially and I guess she assumed I would be able to keep her in the lifestyle she wanted to be accustomed to. I was getting a little concerned about her penchant for wanting to spend my money for her desires, but, sometimes love will blind even the most wary of us all. There were always signs, but I guess love and Elizabeth's presence made me overlook these signs.

She always saw something in a window we passed that she would just "love to have." She seldom came out and asked me to buy things for her, but I knew if I did buy it for her, she would be happy. And everyone wanted to make Elizabeth happy. Didn't we? Life was always better when Elizabeth was happy, and not so good when Elizabeth was disappointed or pouting. She usually got what she wanted.

Eventually we became engaged. Though I had no idea it was going to be the over-the-top engagement party and announcement event of the summer. Which, by the way, she expected me to pay for. I was starting to get a little concerned at this point. Then, one evening, she suggested that I join a country club. It didn't matter to her that I didn't play golf, nor did I have any intention of ever playing golf—what an expensive, silly game. And not just any country club either, she wanted me to join River Run Country Club, the most exclusive one in the county. It was the club where all the "old money" was. Where doctors, lawyers and trust-fund kids played and cavorted, while Hispanics and other minorities brought tall drinks with little umbrellas and fruit in them out to their tables by the pool.

The $25,000 initiation fee to join this club meant nothing to Elizabeth. The fact I didn't play golf meant nothing to her. The only thing that mattered to her was that she become a member and flaunt it to all her friends. Well, that wasn't going to happen. No amount of pouting, no promises of unrestrained love, and no hissy fits would ever change my mind. I was now starting to become seriously concerned about my future with this woman. The final straw for me happened purely by accident.

She was on her computer one night and got a phone call from another up-and-coming socialite. She went into the bedroom so they could share secrets and gossip in private. But, she left her computer on and didn't delete the page she was looking at, which happened to be her account from her bank. I know I probably shouldn't have looked, but I did. She had $50 in her savings account, which was the minimum to keep it active; and her checking account was overdrawn by $3.71. The bank wanted that $3.71 immediately. Apparently, they had sent her two letters telling her she was overdrawn and she still hadn't cleared it up. Uh oh! Great day in the morning, George... someone is trying to scam the scammer.

When she got off the phone, I confronted her about this whole bank mess. I asked her about this big savings account she always referred to, the one she always said she was saving for us to help with our first house together. At first she tried to deny it, then she accused me of spying on her, then she started crying and confessing all sorts of junk—junk I totally didn't care about. What I did care about was someone lying to me and trying to take advantage of me. Heck, that's what I did to people!

I left that night and even though Elizabeth said she would change, I didn't believe her, and truly, I was a bit relieved for it all to be over. Sometimes you just know deep inside when things aren't right. So, no more Elizabeth. At least I protected myself and my assets from that conniving, deceitful aspiring socialite. But she did have great legs!

————

Back to the present day for a moment, I just returned from a treatment for my cancer. I don't know why I continue going to these things. All they seem to do is make me sicker and weaker. If I had enough courage, I'd just stop going, sit home and accept my fate. Eat ice cream and pizza and hamburgers till I pass on to wherever it is I'm going. Where am I going? We all want to go to heaven, but none of us wants to die. However, at this point in my life, death may be a good alternative to what I'll have to go through. Which is: enduring these medical treatments, getting sick, throwing up, losing my hair, losing my sanity and losing my desire to even wake up in the morning. Looking back at my life, it would probably have been much better for everyone (including me) if I'd have just died early. But, it's a little too late to die young now.

Well, I won't be able to drive myself to these so-called treatments much longer anyway, I'm entirely too weak. And, I don't have anyone else who would take me, or want to take me. As you'll soon learn, I seem to have alienated everyone in my life who might have helped me. I really don't mind being alone, my only concern is that I'll die unexpectedly in my home and no one will know about it. I may lie here a week or two before someone figures out I'm dead. I wouldn't like that, not that I would know it. But I wouldn't like it for whoever it was that found me and had to load me in an ambulance. I don't imagine I'd smell too good.

However, I'm sure my death will make several people very happy, and relieve a lot of others, relief that they won't have to deal with me anymore. God is the one person I know who'll talk to me these days, and I like talking to Him. I keep asking Him questions.

He keeps giving me the same answers. My overriding concern now is: Can I believe Him?

Back to my life, such as it was...and is. I enjoyed my job, it wasn't taxing or worrying and I had a very nice income—my savings was really mounting up. But now as I was past 30, I started thinking about a family. Maybe I need a wife to share my life with, to comfort me in my old age. A family to be with on Christmases, birthdays and vacations, all those types of things I see others doing. I should look into that. My problem was that I was enjoying the single life.

Women were plentiful and when I wanted to be alone, I could be alone. If I wanted to go, I could go. If I wanted to eat ice cream and drink beer on Thanksgiving, there was no one to stop me. I was a free American male at the top of my world.

Then Amanda appeared.

11

Amanda had a beauty that couldn't be accurately described—she was just gorgeous. And she never worked at it, or even tried to be beautiful, she just couldn't help it. I met her in the emergency room when I went there for a broken arm. Turns out my arm wasn't broken at all, I'm a bit of a crybaby about injuries. My arm was just bruised, but my heart was completely overwhelmed. Amanda was the nurse on duty that day and when I recovered from her stunning beauty, I first noticed she wore no wedding ring, but maybe she just didn't wear her rings at work. Certainly a goddess like her had to married. My goal was to somehow find out first, if she was married, second, what her name was, and third, how could I somehow get her phone number.

At this point I was almost wishing my arm was broken so I could stay a little longer in the ER. But once the X-rays came back negative, they wanted me out of the way as soon as possible so they could treat patients with real problems. I had little time and no plan and they were already ushering me out the door. Amanda came up to me to give me a prescription for a mild sedative if my arm continued to hurt. I still had no plan. But I knew I could not let this opportunity pass. I figured I had nothing to lose, so I said, "I find you extremely attractive. I don't know if you're married or not, but if not, would you like to get a cup of coffee or something after work?"

Incredibly, she simply said, "Okay", and wrote her phone number on a piece of paper. She then said "I have to go" and she walked away. I must've been in shock, because I didn't move until some orderly tapped me on the shoulder and asked me if I was okay. No, I was not okay, I was love struck. It was only about 2:00 in the afternoon, I didn't know how long she worked or when she got off. Did she mean I could call her today after work? Was this her cell number or home number? Well, I wasn't going to take any chances. I went out to my car and found a better parking spot where I could monitor the exits. I'd sit there and wait for her shift to end. I hope there's not a separate nurse's exit. Do they get off at 4:00, 5:00, 6:00? I had no idea, but I do have a lot of patience. So I waited.

Amanda finally came out of the hospital a little after 7:00. By that time I was on the verge of starving, thirsting to death and wetting my pants. Plus, my arm was killing me since I hadn't filled the prescription or taken any medicine yet. She walked out with three other nurses and I waited till she got to her car, then I called the number she gave me, hoping it was her cell number, not her home number. She answered on the third ring, but it took her a few seconds to remember who I was. She seemed a little surprised by my call. I didn't want to give her the chance to drive away, so I dispensed with the small talk and quickly asked her if she'd like to get a cup of coffee or maybe some dinner (since I was starving). She said "Okay. Where would you like to meet?"

Oh boy, I certainly didn't want her to know I was sitting across the parking lot looking at her. She might think I was stalking her, which by all definitions, I guess I was. I suggested an Italian restaurant nearby that was quaint and dimly lit. She said great and that she'd be there in twenty minutes. Twenty minutes? It was no more than five minutes away, why would it take her twenty minutes? Just shut up and don't ask questions stupid. "Wonderful", I said, "I'll see you then."

The twenty minutes actually worked well for me. It gave me a chance to find a restroom—the first one available, I was in pain. Then I could buy some extra strength Advil (I wouldn't have time to fill the prescription before meeting her). What she did for twenty minutes, I have no idea, but we drove into the parking lot at the same time and she was still in her nurse's uniform—and looked stunning.

We had a nice dinner, shared a bottle of wine—a nice Merlot, and talked and talked and talked. Sensing the waitress really wanted us to move on, we decided to go to the nearest romantic place of all ...Chili's.

It was nearby, they had a bar and we could sit there basically as long as we wanted to—which we did. I would've stayed all night, if it were up to me, but Amanda had an early shift the next day, so she had to leave around midnight.

Should I kiss her goodnight in the parking lot? No, just shake her hand. Shake her hand? What kind of dud are you? Kiss her! I don't want to be too forward. Heck, I don't know what to do...33 years old and I don't know what to do. While I'm mentally playing this senseless game, she quickly leans in, kisses me on the cheek and says "I hope you'll call me again." Don't worry about that Amanda. Don't worry about that AT ALL.

We hit it off immediately. Conversations came naturally, we had similar interests and she was very intelligent and often challenged me with issues and topics other women would never dream of discussing. One new thing with Amanda, she was a Christian and told me early in our relationship that sex would only be after marriage with her. With any other woman I would have probably politely excused myself and moved on, but with Amanda, I knew this was the right thing to do. Heck, not only would I forgo sex, I would've forgone eating, drinking and even breathing if it were possible, if I knew I would have Amanda in the end. She was not only smoking hot, but she was probably the best person I'd ever met as well. I was smitten from the get-go and I've never changed... nearly 40 years later and I still feel the same way. How did things ever get so screwed up? How George? How?

Everything we did with each other was the most fun thing I'd ever done. Go to the movies—best movie I ever saw. Go ice skating— best I've ever skated. Go to dinner—best meal I've ever had. Go running—best run

I'd ever had; etc., etc., etc. She had a way of making everything special, nothing with her was ordinary or mundane. She was everything to me and I knew from that first day in the parking lot at the hospital, this was the woman I wanted to marry and spend the rest of my life with.

We saw each other regularly, every day or two, called several times a day, wrote silly notes and bought each other romantic gifts. I filled her house with flowers. We took several trips together. We went to Bermuda for a few days, Montreal and Quebec City for a week and many day trips to Virginia Beach, but never any sex. I never pushed it and we never had an issue with it. Simply being with her was enough for me.

Amanda had her condo and I had my house and we kept it that way...no living together pre-marriage. She had the effect on me where she could've said, let's give away all our stuff, become missionaries and move to Zimbabwe— and I swear, I think I'd have done it. We did things while dating that I'd never done before; things I didn't want to do and that I would have never done with anyone else. But with Amanda, they were fun. She liked for me to go shopping with her— shopping—which to Amanda meant, you walk around all day looking in store windows. Then, maybe try on a bunch of stuff, but never buy anything except an ice cream cone at the end of the day. And I loved it! (The ice cream helped.)

She wanted me to go to the opera with her. I didn't even know how to spell opera, but I went. The closest

I'd ever been to an opera was watching Elvis, in concert, singing "My Way" at the Norfolk Civic Center two years before. Now, I'm sitting here watching a bunch of middle aged, overweight (not unlike Elvis by the way), over-dressed men and women, sing something in a foreign language, which I don't understand. Being totally perplexed, I look over at Amanda for guidance here, and a tear is rolling down her cheek. Up to that point in my life, it was the most beautiful thing I'd ever seen. If opera could move Amanda to tears, then I loved opera.

I do not understand why—even now—but, Amanda wanted us to go to the Miss Virginia Beauty Pageant that summer. What sort of woman would want to take her boyfriend to a beauty pageant, where he would ogle and drool over the most beautiful women in the state? But we went, we laughed and cut up and had a blast. When they finally announced the winner, these things last forever by the way, I just nodded and applauded with all the others. Knowing that the real Miss Virginia was sitting right next to me and would be forever and ever.

12

Amanda was with me when I got into a fistfight for the only time in my life. I guess you can call one punch a fistfight. I did, and I was proud of it. We decided to spend an afternoon at Virginia Beach, it was a short drive for us and we loved the ocean. Virginia Beach is very nice, clean with wide sandy shores. It's relatively close to a lot of the naval bases in the Norfolk area so there are usually quite a few service personnel there. Though I was never in the service, I have great respect for those young men who do serve and I always try to let them know they have my respect. At the beach, they're usually easy to spot—tattoos, short haircuts, mostly in good physical shape, young and generally very respectful.

This one particular day, we had our little beach chairs sitting out on a fairly crowded area, all sorts of people on the shore that day. Navy guys, old guys, young girls, pretty girls, not so pretty girls and fat, ugly, out of shape, hairy dudes. You can see it all at the beach. We were sitting, lounging, dozing, reading, and I was thinking how lucky I was to be with the most beautiful woman on the entire shore.

Not a care in the known world. Suddenly I heard a kid start screaming. We both looked up and this young guy (maybe mid-20's) grabbed the little kid by the arm and slapped him—hard! The little kid fell to the sand crying and the guy started screaming at him and cursing him—cursing a little kid! I don't know what happened, or what the kid may have done, but this was totally uncalled for and unacceptable.

As the guy continued to scream at the kid, who was now crying uncontrollably in the sand, I stood up, walked over and said "Is everything okay here?" The punk looked at me and said "Mind your own business Pops." Pops? I was probably less than ten years older than this guy. I said, "Look, there's no need to be abusing the kid, no matter what he's done...just calm down." "Oh yeah" he said, he then kicked this little kid right in the stomach. Without thinking, I punched this guy squarely in the nose, blood splattered everywhere. He dropped to the sand like he'd been shot, then he started crying. This overgrown bully was lying in the sand with a bloody nose, crying like a baby and begging me not to hit again. I didn't. I wanted to, but I didn't.

I went back to my chair and sat next to Amanda who had this stunned look on her face. She finally said "My hero" and winked at me. The crying bully finally stopped sobbing. His wife (or girlfriend, or whoever she was—poor girl), gave him a towel to wipe the blood from his nose. Then, they picked up their stuff and left the beach.

As they passed behind us I kept my eye on them to make sure he didn't try to sneak up behind us and sucker punch me. As I was looking at them, the little kid grinned at me and gave me a thumbs up. I think this sorry dude was probably not the kid's real father, maybe he was just the boyfriend of the mother. I'll never know for sure. I'm certain he was not military, he was just an over-grown punk. I would hate to think a father could ever treat his own son like this weak, coward of a man did to that little boy. But, a one punch knockout! I'm 1-0 and plan to stay that way forever.

We met each other's families and, of course, my family loved Amanda. My two worthless brothers were drooling over her and mom and dad thought she was simply perfect. I did too. Does referring to my two brothers as worthless seem cruel to you? Let me explain. Teddy and Frankie were professional loafers. They'd only work long enough to get a little money, then party that money away. They'd then mooch off mom and dad until some unsuspecting employer would hire them again for some menial, meaningless, temporary job where they can earn a few dollars, then start the whole cycle again. Like I said earlier—worthless.

It's hard to understand. They had the same advantages I did, the same educational opportunities I did, the same social networking, the same family, the same everything. But they turned out lazy and unmotivated. I know, I know...talk about calling the kettle black! At least I worked. Dishonestly maybe, but

I did work, their lives simply revolved around mooching and partying.

Disgusting!

Both were athletes in high school, whereas I mostly worked. They did fairly well in the classroom, at least good enough to get accepted into college. However, the college lifestyle only served to reinforce their decadent behavior. Frankie only made it into his second year at George Mason University before he flunked out. He hid it from our parents for close to a year as he lived with friends near campus, partying and playing around. Finally, these so-called friends of his kicked him out because he wouldn't work, help buy food, or pay for any of the expenses. That's when he came back home.

Teddy had a partial scholarship to play tennis at Old Dominion University. It paid close to half the tuition as long as he continued on the team and made decent grades. But the girls, the partying and the freedom of being on his own with no parents to regulate him, was a complete recipe for disaster for him. He finished his freshman year, barely. Then didn't even attempt to go back the next year, what was the point? There were plenty of girls and parties at home and he didn't have to be bothered with going to any classes. And, unfortunately, my parents enabled them both to continue this lifestyle way too long.

They were named after Theodore Roosevelt and Franklin Roosevelt, whom my father greatly admired, as do I. However, neither one displayed any of the traits of their namesakes, such as loyalty, trust, bravery, courage, perserverance and hard work. I was named after George Washington—my dad had great respect for him as well, and since he was the first president, it was only fitting that the first son also be named George. I personally think that I was the favorite child, since I was first born, and I think my parents may have always felt guilty about showing me so much attention. They then over-compensated by letting Teddy and Frankie mooch off them for years.

That's the only explanation I can come up with and since I never was a parent myself. It's something I never understood completely. I know in my mind, they were both waiting for the day when they could inherit some money from mom and dad, I'm sure of that.

Inherit a nice amount of money and live the life of leisure from now on. Well, I took care of that little scenario. I'll explain that later.

Amanda loved my parents and somehow even loved my brothers as well. She had the capacity to see the "good" in people—even in me. It didn't take long for me to realize that my family actually cared more for Amanda than for me, which was totally understandable. My parents secretly wanted a daughter of their own and now they saw the prospect of having one—through marriage hopefully. It was certainly clear my two shiftless brothers would never marry. Even though Teddy now has two children by two different mothers, neither of which wants anything to do with him. Including accepting any child support payments—of which he never offered to pay anyway.

It hurts my parents that they don't get to see their "grandchildren." But Teddy had apparently hurt these women and ruined their lives so completely that they chose to never have anything to do with him again, nor did they want their children to see him or be around him. I guess they were afraid some of Teddy's habits would rub off on the kids.

Now, I was left with the burden of procreating to carry on the family name and heritage. That's a large burden for someone who has previously only wanted to take, never give. But, I was also looking forward to starting a family with Amanda, that is, if she'd ever agree to marry me. I even thought that marrying a wonderful, honest, giving person like Amanda might even change me. I was mistaken—it did not. Wooing Amanda now became my fulltime job with a marriage proposal as my ultimate goal.

———————

I was financially successful, through devious means somewhat. I was charming and funny and everything a woman could want in a man—and not a bit conceited. What would ever prevent this wonderful woman from marrying me? Certainly she knew nothing of my past and we truly loved each other and had wonderful times together. I picked the most perfect occasion and moment to pop the question, though she knew it had to be coming. I planned a 3-day weekend in New York City for us and booked rooms at the Plaza. We went to a Broadway play Friday night, toured some museums on Saturday and had tickets to an exclusive magic show at the Plaza ballroom Saturday night.

I had been planning this for some time, with help from the Plaza and a nice "gratuity" to the magician. Near the end of his performance, which involved help from the audience in several of his illusions, he knew to find his way towards our table and "by mere coincidence" chose Amanda to help him with his next trick. It was an elaborate card trick where Amanda picks a card and the magician does his thing by pulling a fresh orange out of his pocket, telling the audience that the exact card Amanda picked was now magically INSIDE the orange. He asks her to gently peel the orange to reveal the card, but when she does, she finds not a card, but a small box with a ring (from me) and a note that says "Marry me, please!"

I was so thrilled and excited with everything, it turned out exactly how I'd planned it—the perfect proposal. Amanda picked the card, then took the orange from the magician and began peeling it very carefully. Then, she found the little box inside the orange and opened it and read my message. I looked at her, she looked up at me and instead of smiling and beaming her acceptance, she started crying and ran out of the auditorium back to our room, where she locked the door and would not allow me in. Not exactly the script I had planned. The busboy came up to deliver the champagne. I tipped him and kept the bottle, but didn't feel like doing any drinking. I was stunned. I didn't know what to do, except to leave her alone as she asked.

I walked the hallways of the Plaza. I sat in the bar and stared at the walls. I went out and walked the streets with the hobos, pimps and drug dealers. Still, I had no clue what had just happened. After a long, cruel night alone, I finally called the room at daybreak and she answered asking me to come up and see her. I could see the end coming. I was getting ready to lose my Amanda, the only girl I knew I would ever truly love. It was as though I was walking to the gallows. My life would soon be over.

She let me in and I'm quite certain she had also not been to bed that night. It was obviously a traumatic experience for her as well. All I could say to her was "Why?" Then she broke down and started crying again. We held each other for 10 minutes, 20 minutes...I don't know how long. I just know I didn't ever want to let her go.

Finally, she asked me sit down, she had something to tell me. I did not want to hear this, the only time in my life I didn't want to hear that beautiful voice speak. She asked me not to interrupt, to let her tell the whole story, which I did. She told me she loved me with all her heart but could not in good faith marry me. She said she couldn't give me what I most wanted—a family. Amanda told me that in college she'd been sexually assaulted, brutally. The doctors told her she would be unable to bear children as a result of the trauma of this attack. Otherwise, she would heal normally, but her ability to get pregnant was now over.

She told me she knew how much my mom and dad wanted to have grandchildren. How much I'd talked about it and even though she loved me with all her heart, she could not allow me to abandon the hope of children and my future because of her shortcomings. I was stunned. First, I thought "She loves me with all her heart." Secondly I thought "Children? Who cares? I'm not going to lose the most precious thing in the world for some rug rats." No! I told her in no uncertain terms, I did not care about children. I told her my parents' wishes were not part of this equation. The only thing that mattered—the ONLY thing that mattered, was that she loved me and I loved her and I wanted us to be together till the end of time.

Looking back at that now, I only wish that "till the end of time" part had happened.

She agreed to marry me and I thought my heart was going to explode. We fell back onto the bed and hugged and cried and laughed. Then, after ordering room service of blueberry pancakes, bacon and coffee, we started planning our wedding and our lives together.

We decided on a short engagement period. We were ready and didn't want to postpone starting our lives together. Both families were thrilled, mine more than hers. When my parents learned we wouldn't be having any children, they completely understood and, if possible, even loved Amanda more.

My dad called me aside one afternoon when I was visiting them before the marriage. He was uncommonly solemn as he walked me out to the backyard. I had no idea what would be causing him to be so reserved. When we were alone at the back fence he turned to me and said, "George, I have something to tell you that's important to me and I hope you'll find it important as well. I've been waiting all my life to have this conversation with my sons, but it seems as though you'll be the only son I'll have it with. I love Teddy and Frankie, but I seriously doubt they'll ever get married. Lord knows I would feel sorry for the woman who would wed either of them. But you're different, and I feel a responsibility to you and to myself to tell you some things before you get married."

I said, "Sure dad", since I was already aware of the birds and the bees, I had no clue what he wanted to tell me. He continued, "Son, I want you to take this marriage very seriously. You'll only find a woman like Amanda once in your entire life." "I know that dad, don't worry. I'm taking it very seriously and would never hurt Amanda." He said, "I don't think you will either, but you do have a history with women, with some of your relationships not ending well. So I felt I needed to give you this advice. I hope you'll listen to it and think about it."

"I will dad. What is it you want to tell me?" I was amazed and overcome with what he told me. I never forgot that speech the rest of my life. He said, "George, always tell her the honest truth. Don't just be everything she wants, be everything she needs. When she tells you her secrets (and she will), tell her your secrets too. She'll tell you all her hopes and dreams;

you tell them too. When she says she needs you, you tell her you need her too. Always tell her she's beautiful; always tell her the truth. And finally son, when she says she loves you, tell her you love her too." My dad patted me on the shoulder and we walked back inside. He waited a lifetime to tell me that. I remembered it a lifetime.

I went with Amanda to shop for wedding dresses, which was pointless. She was stunningly gorgeous in every dress she tried on. I was in such a good mood that I relented, at my parent's request, and let my brothers be ushers in the wedding. Teddy and Frankie and a few friends decided to throw me a bachelor party, which sounded like a good idea at the time. But an hour or so into it, I snuck out the back door and went home. I was in no mood for any debauchery they had planned. All I could think of was Amanda.

13

We were married in Manassas, Virginia in Amanda's hometown church. Presbyterian by denomination, stuffy and solemn by demeanor. There has never been in the history of weddings a more beautiful bride than Amanda. When she was walking down that aisle towards me I thought I was having a supernatural vision. Something imagined, something that happened only in fairy tales, something only God could create. I was right. We honeymooned in Puerto Rico where the entire week was so perfect, it seems like a dream now. It was so divine that I must've imagined it, but it did happen. We rented a little scooter and rode around the countryside. When we'd find a deserted stretch of beach, we'd pull over and wade into the warm Caribbean surf, Amanda in my arms, love in our hearts and a lifetime of dreams to look forward to. I was indeed the luckiest man on the planet.

We moved into my house, living the dream, thankful to have found each other and looking forward to many, many years of unbridled bliss. I knew I would never cheat on Amanda. No other woman could ever come close to her beauty and passion and nature. She was the only woman on earth for me. There was no one to compare her to. It was totally impossible that I would ever be unfaithful to her. I could never hurt her that way. I would rather die first; but, I am who I am and I couldn't stop my other activities outside the home.

She totally redecorated our home, discarding all remnants of my bachelor past. No more dirty towels in the bathroom, no fishing poles in the corners. There was something else now in the kitchen besides Pop Tarts, Dr. Pepper and cheese-flavored popcorn. It was all fine with me. Everything she did seemed perfect. Even with her ever-changing shift schedule at the hospital and my long work hours, we always made time to be with each other.

We loved going to movies and went once or twice a week. She loved to cook, but it was usually foods that were good for us, not my usual fast food favorites. If it made her happy, I'd eat rocks and dirt. I can't describe those times well enough for anyone to know exactly how I felt. I'm not nearly smart enough to know the right words. I was in love beyond all my comprehension of the meaning of love. I never wanted it to end.

———

My weekend "fishing" trips continued, but I spent a lot of time now thanking God for giving me Amanda. I continued to ask for forgiveness and even asked for guidance and strength to ignore, or fight off, the temptations that always seemed to creep into my life. One afternoon, I was so engrossed in contemplation and in questions and answers that had yet to be clearly defined, or understood—that I neglected to put my fishing pole into the water. I was leaning back, with my eyes closed, wondering about all things eternal, asking God all sorts of questions, when someone suddenly shouts at me, "Hey mister...are you okay"?

Yes Lord, I'm great. I opened my eyes and looked up towards heaven, but all I saw were two good old boys in a beat-up bass boat staring at me from about eight feet away. I said, "Yeah, I'm fine. Thanks for asking." The heaviest of the two (they were both sporting very healthy beer guts), said, "We thought you might be dead."

"Why would you think that?" I replied. "Because you were lying there with your eyes closed, not moving, and your pole wasn't even in the water. We thought you might have had a heart attack or something."

I thanked them for checking on me and assured them I was alright. They offered me a Bud, but I held up a half empty Dr. Pepper and told them I was fine. Good lesson learned. When I'm pretending to be fishing, I need to at least put a line in the water.

The owners of the company I was working for decided they wanted to sell the business and travel. Heck, I'd made them so much money they had no worries forever. They offered me the chance to buy the company from them, if I could somehow arrange the financing. Amanda and I talked it over and decided this kind of opportunity might never come along again. We had to try it. I mortgaged the house (again), borrowed from my dad, even borrowed from Amanda's dad and used the savings Amanda had in her own investments. I could make it work, barely.

The day the deal was done and the money changed hands was one of the scariest of my life. I now owed so much money to so many different people I could not sleep at all that night. Instead, I vowed to never be in this situation again, and, to get out of this debt as quickly as possible, by whatever means it took. And, I do mean "whatever it took". The road to temptation was easy, fast and wide and my brakes really needed adjusting.

The first and most opportune thing I could think of was the cash deposits each week. These had grown to about $1200-1500 each week, of which I was taking about $100-$150 straight into my pocket. Since I now owned the company I wouldn't be cheating anyone except Uncle Sam. I certainly did not declare any of this money as income. Now that I needed to start working on my debt, I started increasing the amount I pocketed each week. It was easy to do because the business was really booming. Our sales were now approaching $4 million a year and each month seemed to out sell the previous month. The little $500 or $700 each week that I was now pocketing was, for all intents and purposes, anonymous. I also granted myself a nice big raise, with moderate raises for my employees. After all, I was the one growing the business...right?

I also upped the sales prices of all items, increased the shipping charges and even added a "handling fee" to the shipments. Nothing I did seemed to curtail sales. After a couple of years I was able to pay off the entire debt and now owned the company outright. I even paid back my dad and Amanda's dad with interest. They were impressed and even talked about "investing" in my little company. But, I was not at the point yet that I wanted to include them in my projects and my business. It was a little shady and I did not need another set of eyes prying into my affairs just yet. I'd keep this business all to myself for the time being.

14

Amanda and I were living the dream. Each day with her was like living in a fairy tale. I couldn't believe how lucky I was to be married to this beautiful, intelligent, fascinating woman. For our first wedding anniversary I had planned to come home from work early, on a Friday afternoon, get all dressed up and take Amanda to a fancy restaurant, then dancing at an upscale club. Amanda had other plans. When I walked in the door, she was waiting on me with two suitcases packed and two envelopes with airplane tickets to Las Vegas. Before I could respond, there was a knock at the door and a limousine driver was there with a limo waiting for us in the driveway.

I couldn't believe this was happening. The limousine driver had drinks prepared for us and a light snack for the drive to the airport. We boarded the first class section and had more drinks and by the time we actually landed in Las Vegas, I could not feel my toes or hands or face—all were numb. Somehow, Amanda got me to the "wedding suite", undressed me and showered me. Then she made sure I could feel the somewhat private parts of my body before I actually passed out that night—or, was it the next morning?

We ordered room service when we woke up. I had no clue what time it was. There was no clock on the nightstand and the windows were so tinted I couldn't tell if was day, or night. But regardless of the time, I knew bacon, strawberry pancakes, eggs, hashbrowns and coffee would be able to clear my head and get me going. A perfect start to the day (or night), all except for one thing— no grits in Vegas. After I'd eaten all I could possibly stuff in my body, Amanda took it upon herself to make sure I forgot about the missing grits. I did.

We went to see Wayne Newton that night. I was surprised by how good he was. We saw Dianna Ross (without the Supremes) the next night. We visited all seven bars in Caesar's Palace and even donated a few quarters to the slot machines. I took Amanda shopping and insisted she buy something nice—not just look around and try stuff on. She finally settled on the slinkiest, sexiest, lowest cut dress they had. She said she'd wear it that night, but would never, ever wear it in Virginia, or in front of any of her friends.

Good! Because the sight of Amanda in that dress would cause other women to faint, little kids to run crying to their mama, and make grown men fall on their hands and knees and start howling at the moon! Trust me.

———

We both worked hard at getting the debt was paid off. Neither of us felt comfortable owing so much money. It really didn't take us as long as I thought it would to pay it all off. When we finally owed no more money, then we started enjoying ourselves. I wanted to make her wishes come true, so, we travelled to places Amanda had always dreamed of: France, South Africa, Australia and Polynesia.

We even discussed buying a small apartment in New York City, since we loved visiting there so much. She loved experiencing things and seeing things she'd read about in school...the Louvre, Notre Dame, Versailles, the Eiffel Tower in Paris. Sydney and Melbourne Australia, the Great Barrier Reef, Ayers Rock, the Rock of Gibralter. All these things totally excited her. Me, I could've had a good time lying on the beach, dozing, sipping a Dr. Pepper and knowing I had the prettiest woman in the world lying next to me. Everything else was just a bonus.

Amanda still loved nursing. It was in her nature as a caring and giving person, and didn't want to give up her career. Even after it became apparent I could support us both very well, she still wanted to work and I never argued with her about it. I always gave her everything she wanted, except in the end, the truth. I would usually "write off" these trips as business expenses, it was much easier on the taxes that way and since there was no one else looking at my books except my accountant. He was certainly not going to question anything from one of his largest customers.

Amanda loved visiting New York. She loved the cultural aspects of the museums and galleries. We loved going to Broadway shows and off-Broadway shows. There were always multiple things to choose from in New York. We loved the place and thought seriously several times of moving there. But to do that, I would have to hire someone to oversee the daily operations of my business. And, that was not going to happen—not yet anyway.

On one of our trips to the city, Amanda had an appointment one morning at a spa, so I was left alone and ended up at an upscale coffee shop. You know the kind: yuppies in bow ties, women with their noses stuck up in the air, and coffee with so much crap added to it that it's not even coffee any longer. When I ordered a regular coffee, it's like I insulted them. In reality, I'm the one who should be insulted by paying $4.95 for a cup of Joe!

When I got my overpriced cup of bland tasting coffee I couldn't help but overhear (everyone in the place couldn't help but overhear) a woman who was upset that her café mocha latte with two shots of expresso wasn't exactly the way she ordered it. Was it too hot to sip it? Was it not non-fat? She started screaming at the young girl behind the counter, and I could tell this girl really wanted to punch this woman in the face, but she didn't. She simply said, "I'll get you another one for free and I hope you have a nice day."

It didn't stop this woman. She continued to berate the poor girl and everyone who worked there. Finally, unable to bear it any longer, the man in line behind the abusive woman said, and I quote, "Lady, it's just a fucking cup of coffee." Everyone in the place erupted in applause and the woman stormed out without her double shot of expresso, capped off with a mocha latte bull crap. Sometimes you have to be proud of your fellow man and disgusted with your fellow woman.

I'm off track. After this very amusing incident, I was sitting there still smiling inside when a guy at the next table started discussing the incident with me and we both began laughing about it. He was very amiable and easy to talk to. We discussed sports, politics, women, coffee, foreign affairs, his wife, my wife and everything in between.

I was very happy to find someone with some common sense to sit and talk to while Amanda was at the spa.

Mike was very funny, very intelligent and we became instant friends. He lived in New Jersey, but said he had an office in New York and was in the "investment business". From the way he was dressed and talked, I figured he was very successful. It certainly seemed like it.

We started talking business and investments and opportunities and he started telling me about some "wonderful opportunities" he had coming up that I might be interested in. When he started telling me the return rates of his investments I became extremely interested. They were higher than any rates you would normally find at banks, brokers or financial planners, that's for sure. He was very close to the vest on exactly how his business worked and what he invested in to get such high returns. I could understand that, he didn't want others to horn in on his business or take away any part of it. Mike had me hooked and he knew it.

He was offering short term investments with high rates of return. The stipulation being that all investments to him were to be made in cash and that all payments from him back to you were made in cash. It was a "trust business" he said, with high rewards for those trusting enough to take advantage of it. You had to trust him and him alone and he would ensure your equity and returns. Talk about shady deals...this one was gift wrapped in tinsel with a big card that read "DO NOT OPEN"! I took his card and told him I'd think about it.

We walked outside and he had a Mercedes, with a driver, waiting on him. That's a good way to impress people. I took my plain black coffee, refilled for only $2.99, back to the hotel, waited for Amanda and started thinking about what I'd just heard.

———

I had always been a little concerned about depositing so much cash from my business each week in the bank. I didn't want to raise any eyebrows, or, have people start saying "Isn't it odd that George Kerry keeps depositing $1000 a week in cash into his account?"

I did not ever want anyone to have those thoughts, so, I started putting most of my cash into safe deposit boxes. I had three big boxes in different banks around town that I put cash in. Those boxes would hold a lot of

$100 bills. I deposited some of the cash in my accounts, but not every week and certainly not a high percentage of it.

I had a lot of cash and really no way to invest it legally without raising question marks. That's why Mike's venture had a great appeal to me. That, and because it seemed a bit underhanded and not exactly kosher—if you know what I mean. I can't adequately explain it, but I've always been drawn to the underside of things, the shady areas, the questionable practices. I don't know why. I didn't need any more money. I was doing great as is, but the appeal of something a tad murky just grabbed my attention and wouldn't let go.

Amanda and I had our usual great time in New York, but Mike certainly had caught my attention. After returning home, I called him several times, asking questions, just trying to get a feel from him on the type person he was and what he was offering. He was genial and friendly, but was not going to give out any details of his business. I either had to trust him, or not trust him. As you can probably guess, I ended up trusting him. I was leery and didn't want to jump in with both feet, I just wanted to dip my little toes in the water and get a feel for the temperature.

Unfortunately for me, the minimum deposit Mike would work with was $5,000. Now, $5,000 was not going to break me, but it's still a lot of money to give someone with no collateral and nothing but their word that everything would be fine. It was a ninety day unwritten contract, and at the end of those ninety days, I could expect to see a 20% return on my investment.

Most banks offered about 2–3% a year. If you were lucky in the market you might make 10–15% a year, so this 20% each quarter seemed fantastic. It was.

At the end of the first ninety days, I met Mike and he gave me an envelope with $6,000 cash in it—a twenty percent increase on my investment. Great, let's try this again. I next invested $10,000 with Mike and ninety days later got $12,000 back in my envelope. I was hooked. I didn't wait for the ninety day period to end before investing more, I started investing about $10,000 each month or so.

I would usually have anywhere from $30,000–$50,000 invested at any one time. I do not know what Mike did with the money. I never asked any more questions and he never volunteered any answers.

I only know that he was never late with any payments to me and that I never wanted to meet any of his "delivery men" in a dark alley. I would usually drive up I–95 for two or three hours and meet one of Mike's guys at a rest stop or gas station. They'd say hello, talk about traffic or the weather, then hand me the envelope and we'd be on our way. They were dressed nicely, but obviously had spent a lot of money on steroids and gym memberships. I would never punch any of these guys in the nose, no matter what they did.

It didn't take long before I had to find more safe deposit boxes, the large ones. It was surprising how fast they fill up with hundred dollar bills. This was obviously not something I shared with Amanda. The safe deposit boxes and the way they were filled was to be my little secret...she would never understand this. I used some of this money for dinners, gas, clothes, movies, things like that, but it was hard to spend even a fraction of what I was getting each month. I was filling up safe deposit boxes all over town now. Except for investing with Mike, I really didn't have a plan with what I would do with all this cash money. I just know I liked having it, in case I ever needed it for anything.

I bought a car once and paid cash for it. I mean I paid for it with $100 bills. I shouldn't have done that. It created too much talk in the dealership and that's the last thing I wanted—someone talking about George Kerry and all this cash he had. I wasn't thinking. I let my desire for this car I wanted, and a need to "use" some of this money, alter my sense of privacy and security. But it was a sweet car...the biggest, most luxurious and expensive SUV Cadillac made. It was almost like driving a customized tank down the road. Amanda didn't really care for it, but I loved it.

15

Amanda and I had been discussing about what we wanted to do for our wedding anniversary. We looked at travel brochures, we read magazines, but we just couldn't decide on something that really excited us. Then, one night on television we saw a commercial for a movie being filmed in Florida. There was a chase scene on the highway from Miami leading to the Keys—the road where it's only two-lanes, with the ocean on both sides. Amanda didn't really like the movie, but she thought the highway looked great! She said, "I've always dreamed of driving on that road." I replied, "You dreamed of that road?" She looked at me said, "George, people who don't have dreams, don't have much." She wanted us to drive on that road from Miami to Key West for our anniversary, and you should know by now, that anything Amanda can dream, I can deliver.

I told her I'd look into plane reservations the next day..."No", she said, "We have your new car. Let's drive down there and visit some places on the way." "What places?" I said. I didn't know there was anything worth visiting on the way to Florida. I immediately saw a light turn on in her face—"Charleston, Savannah, Atlanta, Cape Canaveral, Orlando, Disneyworld, Saint

Augustine" she was rattling off places so fast you'd have thought Alex Trebek was testing her. "You want to visit all those places, and go to Key West?" "Yes!" she said. "Well, maybe not all of them, but it'll be great George. You're gonna have fun!" All I could do was look at her and say, "Honey, as long as I'm with you, I'll always have fun."

We hit I-95 and headed south. As soon as we crossed the border into North Carolina we started seeing signs for "South of the Border." Stop and visit Pedro. Eat with Pedro. Gas up with Pedro.

Play games with Pedro. Before we even got there, we were a bit over-dosed on Pedro, but Amanda had to see the place, so we stopped. We shouldn't have. Except for having inexpensive gas, we weren't that excited about Pedro's. But being the good amigo he was, on billboards for the next 20 miles, he kept thanking us for stopping and urging us to turn around and "Come Back." We didn't.

Amanda wanted to us to visit Charleston, which of course we did. She fell in love with all the Spanish moss hanging from the oak trees down at The Battery and around the countryside. We took the tour boat out to Fort Sumter, which I found fascinating, and we shopped at the Moon Pie General Store. Amanda saw a flier for a 5K run on Saturday, so we stayed an extra day so she could do the run over the gorgeous Ravenel Bridge across the Cooper River. We liked Charleston, more than I thought we would, but we had to keep moving.

We stopped in Savannah and took a ghost tour that night. I thought it was a little weird, and Amanda found it a tad bit "spooky." The next morning we shopped on River Street and Amanda bought a painting of an old abandoned boat, tipped on its side, with the sun setting behind it, and had it shipped to our house. We took a cruise on a river boat down the Savannah River, while dining on some of the best seafood I've ever eaten. Amanda loved it here and we couldn't decide which place we liked more...Charleston or Savannah.

I was beginning to doubt if we'd ever make it to the Keys. She wanted us to stop at St. Augustine, which we did...,no comment. She decided we didn't have enough time to visit Disneyworld, but she insisted we stop at Cape Canaveral and take a tour. I'm glad we did that, it was indeed wonderful.

We didn't stop again until we got to Miami, where we got a room at South Beach, directly on the ocean front, and yes, it was expensive. However, the sight of Amanda in a bikini wading in the surf was worth any amount of money that hotel charged us. We had fruity concoctions at the hotel bar that night, and walked barefoot down the beach, holding hands and sipping our tall, icy, Cuban drinks.

Finally, the next day we headed towards Key West, on the road we'd seen on TV, miles ahead of us with nothing but ocean surrounding us. Then a tropical storm comes in. Not a big one, but big enough so that it was scary driving on that ocean road. High waves in the sea, with rain and wind lashing our car.

Amanda liked my big SUV now, I did too. We finally made it to Key West and the storm blew out to sea. We'd stopped so often on the way down that we could only stay there two days before we had to leave. But in those two days we must've shopped in every store in that little town. I'm sure we had drinks in every bar Hemingway supposedly drank in, and even visited the great author's house (and saw his six-toed cats).

When we left for home, the drive back on the ocean road was everything Amanda had hoped it would be, and just as beautiful as it was on TV that night. But... not nearly as beautiful as the woman sitting next to me in my new, fully-loaded, white, Cadillac SUV.

———————

My dad had started having health problems about this time. It started with some physical pains, then annoying lapses of memory. Then more severe memory lapses, then total Alzheimer's symptoms set in. He was too young for this, but isn't everyone? Even though he and mom had invested well and saved enough to last their entire lives, they never expected Mr. Alzheimer to visit them and never leave.

Some days, dad would seem okay for awhile. Others, he wouldn't recognize who I was. Mom caught him paying the same bills twice, or even three times. She finally had to hide the check book when she saw that he had written one check for $4,500 to the Virginia Symphony and another for $2,995 to the Wilderness Society. Dad never listened to symphony

116

music and his idea of wilderness was the undeveloped land out behind the new Walmart.

Soon, mom couldn't take care of dad any longer and he needed full-time attention and moved into a nursing home. Those places are not cheap.

At about $6,000 a month, it doesn't take long to completely run through your savings. Mom was blindsided by the costs and never knew what hit her. By the time she got me to "look into things," they had lost over ¾ of their life savings. That's when I took over. Dad had always handled their finances and mom knew very little of how it all worked.

They didn't have a lot of investments, mostly a few mutual funds which mom was selling off to pay for dad's care. They were living off dad's retirement and their social security checks, which was plenty enough for them—before dad got sick. I convinced mom to assign me as guardian and got their power of attorney as well. She knew she could trust me, and that I knew how to handle money. I now had full control of their finances and I was going to make sure I turned this thing around.

Immediately, I invested their money with Mike and within the year I had increased their savings back to a level that wasn't worrying mom any longer. Once it got back to the point where they had more than they had before, my old habits kicked in. I just can't seem to help myself. Instead of giving mom the full 20% each ninety day period, I would only give her 10% and I'd keep the other 10% for myself. Sounds terrible I know, but still, my mom was making a 40% increase on her investments yearly...40%! And, if they'd needed the other 40% for any reason, I would've given it to her.

Since this whole scheme was done in cash, I still had to be careful with mom's cash deposits. I didn't want to attract any attention. So, to keep under the radar of any bank auditors, I kept half of her profits in safe deposit boxes and only deposited smaller amounts of cash in her accounts. Soon, mom was paying for dad's care, while growing her bank account, all thanks to my friend Mike.

The best thing about this whole deal, if there is a best thing about your dad being unable to recognize you any longer, was that I now had power of attorney. I was able to change all the wills my parents had that included my good-for-nothing brothers. I completely cut them out of everything, except to leave them each $50 to go out and have a farewell meal. Farewell...which is what I knew it would be when they found out what I'd done. It was completed legal and within the boundaries of good conscience on my part. They would never be able to contest the will in court.

Mom signed it. Our attorney signed it and I signed it as legal heir. Mom was concerned about it. She couldn't stop loving her two babies, but she also did not want them to get dad's money and blow it on their increasingly decadent lifestyle. She did ask me if I would look after them and if they truly needed something. Would I help them? Sure mom, I'll help them. I was sick and tired of them mooching off my parents, taking "loans" from them with no intention of ever paying them back. I'd make sure "Frick and Frack" got exactly the kind of help that was coming to them.

Frankie had a drug problem and had been arrested several times for minor violations. I told him to never call me expecting help if he got arrested again, and he didn't. However, he did call mom.

Unfortunately for Frankie, I now controlled mom's money and I refused to bail him out or pay for anything he needed, including a lawyer.

He pleaded with mom for help. She pleaded with me. Amanda pleaded with me. This was the only time I remember I could not give Amanda what she asked for. I just couldn't do it. Amanda understood, but her heart was so big she still wanted to help Frankie, but bailing him out over and over was not helping. Sooner or later Frankie had to learn to help himself, to take responsibility for his actions, to answer for his deeds. As far as I was concerned, that time was now.

I truly don't know how my other brother, Teddy, lived. He seldom worked, he had no apartment or house of his own and he drove a beat-up used car. Yet he always seemed to have enough money to buy liquor, or whatever else kept him going. He could always weasel his way into staying with some woman he'd just met in a bar. He was a good looking guy, but his lifestyle was taking a toll on him. He looked about ten years older than he really was.

Occasionally, when we met for some reason, he would ask me if he could "borrow" a few dollars. I hate to admit this, but I would give him $20 or $30 from time to time. I shouldn't have. I know this was only enabling his lifestyle, but Teddy was so likeable and had so much potential. It just broke my heart to see what was happening to him.

Teddy was the guy in high school who was captain of the basketball team, dated the head cheerleader, was everybody's best friend and was the most likely to succeed. He just never did. He used people. And even though people knew he was using them, they let him use them anyway. They couldn't help but love the guy. He always had multiple girlfriends, was always either just coming from a party, or just going to a party— heck, he WAS the party. If you were with Teddy, it was guaranteed you were going to have a good time.

All this worked great in school and when you're young. It starts to become a concern as you age, and then becomes a legitimate nightmare into your adult years. Still, you just couldn't help but love the guy. Women wanted to take care of him. Mom wanted to coddle him. Dad wanted to mentor him. Amanda wanted to nurse him. Frankie wanted to hang around with him. And me—I wanted to hug him, then smack him back to reality and kick him out in the street at the same time. Sometimes, family is hard.

16

Outside of work acquaintances and family, I had no one you would consider a friend. I didn't play golf, or tennis, or enjoy going to ballgames with the "guys." I still enjoyed fishing, or what Amanda thought was fishing, I thought of it more as "solituding" than fishing. I seldom caught anything, because I didn't try to catch anything. I was more interested in the alone time sitting in a small boat in the middle of a lake with no one else around me.

Somehow, these "alone times" seemed to clarify things for me, to put things in perspective. I know this will seem weird to you, but I felt I could communicate with God out on the lake all alone. I didn't really know God, but He knew me. Alone on the lake, I felt He knew all my secrets and all my dirty dealings and all my desires and yet, I felt He still loved me. Amanda loved me, but she didn't know all about me. God KNEW all about me and still loved me. That's why the lake was important to me—not for the fishing, but for the love.

I was fairly friendly with a guy I met who was an insurance agent in town; he sold me life insurance and car and home insurance. He seemed like a nice guy and didn't ask too many questions about my business or my personal life. His wife and Amanda were best buddies, or whatever the term is for women. We would go out to dinner with them every week or two, maybe to a concert or a day at the beach—things that made Amanda happy. Honestly, I was completely and 100% happy and content with just me and Amanda.

I didn't need anyone else, or particularly want to be with other people. But she thought it would be nice for me to have a "pal," so I tried. It didn't turn out well.

This guy's name was Christopher, but for some reason he went by CJ. I don't know why and was never interested enough to ask him.

He always wanted to talk about sports—golf tournaments, ball games, things I had absolutely no interest in. He would bore me to tears with who won what and how many points someone scored, who was on first, what was on second and I don't give a crap who was on third. Sorry for my language, but I had to endure this nonsense and pretend to enjoy his company. I'm not good at pretending.

Amanda convinced me to go to the ocean one weekend with CJ and his wife. "We'll have fun" she said. "You'll get to know CJ better" she said. "They're a joy to be around" she said. As far as I know, Amanda never lied to me our entire lives, but this was close. I didn't want to get to know CJ better. They were not a joy to be around. In fact, CJ's wife treated him like dirt, and the only fun I had (except the nights alone with Amanda) was Saturday when CJ and I signed up for a deep sea fishing trip while the girls went shopping.

I didn't actually have fun because of the fishing, which was relatively boring since no one caught anything bigger than a 12" mackerel. I had fun because CJ had bragged to me about always going out on the ocean with his buddies and gloating about how he never got seasick. He made a point of telling everyone how he didn't need any Dramamine or patches, or anything else. By god, he grew up on the ocean.

Well, old CJ had a rude homecoming on his ocean. He started getting dizzy on the way out. He threw up his breakfast before we stopped. He threw up last night's dinner before we started back and then he threw up last week's pepperoni pizza before we docked. He was a sick, little puppy. I was proud of myself for not gloating and even acted like I felt sorry for him when the girls met us. I didn't.

After the ocean escapade, CJ kept hinting that he really liked fishing in lakes and rivers better than the deep sea fishing anyway. He was trying to get me to invite him to come with me on one of my lake trips. That was not going to happen. While his wife and Amanda would do girl stuff, we'd hang around or bum around, just basically doing nothing...passing time until the girls came back.

Somehow, he enjoyed this—it bored the daylights out of me! The conversations were interminable; the subject matter was dull, lifeless, monotonous, stupid, tedious, tiresome, trite and totally uninteresting. Do you get my drift?

CJ would ask me to golf with him—NO. Go bowling with him—NO. Go to the ballgame with him—NO. Couldn't this guy take a hint? Didn't he have any other friends? Well, eventually I found the reason he wanted to talk to someone—me, in particular. He suspected his wife was running around on him and he wanted to see if Amanda knew about it and had told me anything. If she did know, she never said a word to me and I never suspected anything, or cared, anyway. CJ's wife was not the kind of woman you'd expect to be having an affair. She was fairly flat-chested, plain and a little plump. But guess what? This little plain Jane was not only having an affair, she was having two affairs simultaneously—each unbeknownst to the other poor slob.

When it all blew out into the open, it was an ugly mess for them. Fortunately they didn't have any children, apparently the result of CJ never having sex with his wife. Which, according to her, was the reason she HAD to resort to all the affairs in the first place. Go figure. Anyway, Amanda ended her friendship with Lolita, but CJ kept calling me and calling me, wanting to "talk." Lord have mercy. I would meet him and listen to his sad story over and over and over. Truly, I felt sorry for him, but I did not have time for him to keep crying on my shoulder.

Finally, enough was enough; I agreed to meet him again for lunch one day, but this was going to be the last meeting for me. I couldn't take it any longer.

Before we even ordered, he started in with the same old crap when I stopped him cold. "Listen CJ" I said "I'm sick to death of hearing about all this. Get over it! That woman does not love you and seemingly never will. Quit crying about it, move on with your life and most importantly, leave me out of it." I guess I could've been a little more sensitive, but there comes a time when you just can't take it anymore. This was one of those times. I never heard from CJ again, and the next day I changed insurance agents.

———————

Amanda had plenty of nurse friends and friends from all the various activities and organizations she was involved in. She would meet them for lunch, for shopping, for drinks, for whatever it is women do when they gather. A lot of that is still a mystery to most men. Occasionally, we would meet some of her friends together, I always agreed because I was totally unable to say no to anything Amanda asked me. As long as she was with me, I could endure almost anything, especially if I knew it made her happy.

We also enjoyed spending time with her parents. Amanda was an only child and her parents doted on her and loved it when we visited. Amanda's dad was always interested in my business and always asked a lot of questions, which I tried to deflect as much as possible. After my dad's sickness, he learned from Amanda that I had invested mom's money to get her out of financial trouble. He knew something of the investment returns mom was making, not any specifics, but he was interested in checking this out. I should've kept this all a much better secret.

I thought about this long and hard and finally decided I did not want to take the chance of him finding out anything about my investments with Mike. Or even worse— losing any money with Mike. It would be very difficult for me to explain this to Amanda and I didn't want to take that chance. Privately, I told Amanda's dad that it was just stock investments that I had and that I was personally supplementing my mom's account from my own savings. He liked that. He was a bit disappointed that he couldn't get in the sweet deal he thought I had, but he understood. Whew!

Amanda's dad had done well financially. He and his wife were very comfortable...not rich, but comfortable. He had never invested in the stock market. He had a few government bonds (which paid next to nothing), and he had some land he was going to sell; but he knew nothing about investing in the market. Now, since he thought I was a stock guru, he wanted me to help him with some investments. It took several weeks for me to commit to help him. I just did not want to ever be put in a position where it could affect the way Amanda felt about me.

I finally agreed to help, with Amanda's urging. I had several stocks I'd had for quite some time that had always performed well, 10-12% gains usually. Amanda's dad didn't know the first thing about buying stocks, so he just gave me his money and I bought the stocks through my account for him. I know what you're thinking, but I NEVER took any of his money. What I did do was only buy stocks that paid quarterly dividends, and then I'd keep the dividends each of these stocks paid out. I figured that was my fee for the services I was providing. Each quarter the stocks I bought for him paid a total of about $1,200 in dividends. No one else knew these stocks paid quarterly dividends and as long as Amanda's dad was making money (which he was), then everyone was happy. Famous last words.

Everything seemed to be rolling along fine. My business was still doing very well, my stock investments were increasing—the future seems unlimited. Then, I get a phone call from Mike. Can I meet him tomorrow? It's important. Well, when someone is holding over $125,000 of your mom's money and your money, the answer is YES, I'll meet you anywhere, anytime. I pulled in the rest area where we usually met and Mike was there waiting for me. No deliverymen this time, just Mike, which was very unusual. Except for meeting him that first day in the coffee shop, I'd only met Mike in person one other time. I could tell he was nervous and not his usual confident self. I knew this meeting was not going to be something I wanted to hear.

He said the Feds were checking him out (whatever that means).

He was going to have to lay low for awhile and cease the "investment scheme" until further notice. He then handed me a large grocery bag full of cash, which he said was my investments to date—all of it. He told me he kept no written records and no names were written down anywhere. I had nothing to worry about, and that he'd call me when things were okay to resume the operation.

Well, I never heard from Mike again. I don't know what happened to him, if anything did. I did not dare call his phone number, for fear the "Feds" would be monitoring it. In fact, I burned his card and immediately started thinking of how I could replace this "lost income" of mine. However, my main priority now was taking care of mom. My dad finally succumbed to the effects of Alzheimer's and old age and I had to make sure mom could live comfortably in the future.

Losing my dad was tough. You only have one dad your entire life. When he's gone, it takes a while to accept the reality of it and realize you don't have him there any longer to help you out, or listen to you, or give you advice. I fished a lot the next few weeks. I thought of Dad, I thought of God, I thought of Amanda and I thought of myself. I wondered if any of these other people love me if they knew the real me? Would any of them forgive me if they knew the real me?

The problem I have, as I see it, is that I CANNOT change who I am on the inside. I can change my appearance. I can change my location. I can change my relationships, but I can't change myself any more than a drowning person can save himself. Maybe I'll change fishing poles.

Out on my boat one cloudy, overcast summer day, I read a passage in the Bible that says "The human

heart is the most deceitful of all things, and
desperately wicked." That's an eye-opener! And
furthermore, there's nothing I can do to change this
fact, or change myself. I'm hoping that somehow God
can change my heart and change my life. It is
possible...isn't it? Another passage I read later said
that the Devil is like a roaring lion, searching for
whomever he might devour. Am I like the devil? I'm
always searching for a way to devour something or
someone on a financial deal. Surely (hopefully) I'm not
like the devil. I close my eyes and pray, "Please Lord,
give me a sign that I'm not the devil."

Fifteen seconds later—BOOM! A bolt of lightning
strikes the water about fifty yards from my boat. My
hair stands on end and the air crackles around me. All
the other fishermen hurry for shore. I'm still
bewildered, shocked and breathless...and I think I wet
my pants. I finally gather my wits enough to start back
for shore as the air rumbles overhead and the wind
suddenly picks up. When I make it to the landing and
get out of the boat, I quietly look up into the sky and
say, "Okay Lord, but can you give me a different sign?"

I think I'll fish in some deeper water.

17

With my dad's retirement and her Social Security, mom was pretty well set. The money I had "invested" with Mike for her was just a bonus. All the same, I did not want my two loafing brothers to get their hands on any of mom's money. Since I had Power of Attorney now, I and I alone, decided how her money was spent. I decided how she invested her money and how her life insurance policies were handled.

Before dad died I changed his policies to leave everything to mom, except for the $50 apiece to Frankie and Teddy. They were extremely unhappy with this, but there was nothing they could do except cry to mom. They actually thought they were "owed" that money, that dad had promised it to them. Well boys, here's a new promise: I promise you'll never get another red cent from mom as long as I'm alive; go get a job and make your own money. Quit expecting mom, or anyone else to take care of your sorry loafing selves. They pledged long and loud, "We'll get you for this George." They didn't need to, I'd get myself soon enough.

Soon after dad died I finally talked mom into moving into a "retirement village" for senior adults.

She'd be around people her own age, all meals would be prepared for her, plenty of activities were available and the staff was around to check on her at all times. We found a gorgeous place nearby. A three room apartment that was really all she needed, if not a bit too much. Plus, it was only for residents, meaning my two sorry brothers could forget about ever moving in with her. We sold her house pretty quickly and now my two siblings had to figure out what they were going to do since they couldn't freeload off mom any longer.

I must admit, even though I did have mom's best interest in mind, I also planned this to specifically cut off any thoughts Frankie and Teddy had of mooching off mom any longer. They were now on their own. They each approached mom about getting "small loans" to help them find apartments to live in. She told them all her finances were being handled by me. That was the last thing they wanted to hear. Instead of asking me for a "loan", they instead went behind my back and approached Amanda. Well, Amanda may have a big heart and see the good in people, but she wasn't stupid. She knew my brothers well now and she knew what I would say, they were out of luck.

When everything settled back down a bit, Amanda decided we needed to get away and do something exciting. Her view of exciting was completely different from my view of exciting. For me, exciting meant that I'd drink a Mountain Dew instead of a Dr. Pepper in my boat that day. Those Dews can pack quite a kick! Amanda's view of exciting was a little more extreme, in this case, skiing in Colorado.

Had we ever been skiing before? No. Did we own any skis? No. Was this going to deter Amanda? Big, fat NO.

I said, "Colorado? Couldn't we just try it here in our little Appalachian Mountains?" She looked at me like a mother would look at her six year old son who was asking why he had to take a bath that night, and said, "We're going to Colorado, we're going to ski, and you're going to have fun. Do you understand?" "Umm, yes ma'am." So, we flew to Denver, rented a car and drove up to Breckenridge, a little ski resort nestled amongst several 14,000 foot peaks. My little 3,000 foot comfortable looking mountains in Virginia seemed pretty reassuring right now. However, I liked the little town of Breckenridge. It had a stream running through it, little shops and cafes, a Rastafarian Pasta restaurant and a crepe stand on Main Street that made the sweetest, tastiest crepes you've ever tasted— all made to order.

We found skis at the rental place and checked in our condo for the week. We looked out the rear deck and there was the ski lift right there at our back door. It would take us up to the top of the mountain...incredible! New skis, fresh powder, ski lift at our back door, what more could we ask for? How about, actually knowing how to ski? They had something called a "bunny slope" which was supposed to be for beginners to learn on. Honestly, it went straight downhill. It would've scared the daylights out of Jean Claude-Killy. I'm not exaggerating.

Amanda, being a much better athlete than I ever was, took to it immediately. Pretty soon, she graduated from the bunny slopes to the intermediate slopes and beyond. I didn't even want to know how to spell "intermediate". On the bunny slopes, I would sort of ski sideways to the other side of the slope (not down the hill). Then I'd fall down (I never learned how to stop effectively), get back up and ski sideways to the other side of the slope. Then fall down again, get up and keep doing that all the way down. It was a tremendous cardio workout for me falling down and getting up all day. The only enjoyable moments for me came when riding the chair lift back to the top.

It passed by all the condos, which were built on the side of the mountain all the way to the top. You could look in the back doors of all these condos. I saw naked people, usually young, ugly college guys. I saw people eating breakfast and lunch, I saw people having drinks. One couple even tried to hand me a glass of something as I rode by them—unsuccessfully, I'm afraid. I saw babies crying and lovers kissing and old people sleeping. Then, the ski lift reached the top and dumped me on the ground.

I never did learn how to exit the lift properly. It doesn't stop, it just makes a turn and you're supposed to "ski off" towards the slopes. Amanda was really good at this exiting and skiing off part. I was good at sitting in a boat, eating sardines and burping. Once, I almost made it out without falling. After that, I just gave up, let it dump me on the ground and tried not to look too embarrassed in front of all the other bunny-slopers.

And even with all this, it was still fun. Why? Because Amanda loved it!

She was a natural and stayed on the slopes all day. I'm sure she only stopped because of me, or else she'd have stayed all night, since the slopes were lit at night. As she came down from her last run of the day, my anticipation started growing. I knew the crepe place was nearby, the Breckenridge Brewing Co. was still open and I would get to eventually go to bed with the hottest ski mama on the whole mountain. Just be patient George.

18

With her retirement check and her Social Security mom could easily pay the monthly fees for the retirement home. She was set for life. Now it was time for me to put her savings to work for us all. I had been approached by some guys I dealt with locally about starting a small side business. It intrigued me because I now had some excess capital to work with and the idea they had really appealed to me. They wanted to finance a small clinic catering to lower income families, specifically the Hispanic population which was now booming in our city.

My two partners were financially sound and secure (I checked them out), plus, I knew them in a social setting sort of way. Amanda and I knew Don from several of the hospital charities and functions we attended. Every time I saw him at any event, I mean EVERY time, he had on a different, multi-colored, checked, striped or patterned sports coat. Usually with a flamboyant tie and slacks as well, and he wore spats on top of it all. This guy must've had over a hundred sports coats and a room full of accessories. He was wild, flashy, ostentatious, and knew every joke and tall tale ever invented, but had a business savvy as keen as anyone you'll ever meet. He wanted people to think he was goofy. Then he'd make a deal that would take all your money before you knew what happened. I had to be careful with Don.

Ralph was completely opposite of Don, he was almost invisible. He seldom spoke, never wore a coat and tie—only blue jeans and boat shoes (no socks), never told a joke, and never smiled (to my knowledge). But he carried a big financial stick, and he used it to acquire businesses and sell businesses—always to his financial gain. These were two of the "big boys" and I had to be careful in my partnership with them. As nice as they could both appear to be, each one of them would cut your heart out if it would gain them an extra dollar.

Don and Ralph had done some research and figured out we could hire a couple of doctors fresh out of medical school. The guys who weren't at the top of their class, and weren't receiving offers from the big hospitals. We'd give them a decent starting salary, hire a P.A. and a nurse or two who spoke Spanish and start our own clinic. We already had a built in customer base and a government which seems willing to pay for any medical procedures needed for our minority population, whether they're legal or illegal.

All that was needed was the financing to get the building and equipment to get started. Seems simple, but there were a lot of hoops to jump through. The licenses and permits alone would almost drive us crazy; and the cost of the medical equipment needed was astronomical. But I knew I could get loans for this, I had a good reputation and plenty of collateral. Plus, if I could arrange most of the financing, then, I could be the one in control and thus, be the one who benefits most from the profits.

I discussed the whole thing with Amanda, since she was an expert in the medical field. First, was there a need for such a clinic? Yes, she said, the hospital emergency rooms are over-flowing with people needing help, but who don't have any doctor to go to. Can we expect to see a decent return on our investment? Of course, Amanda told us that city, state and federal governments cover nearly all costs now for those who don't have enough insurance coverage.

We knew that new Federal regulations were in place to ensure that everyone had health care, but the sad fact was that most immigrants (legal and illegal) had no coverage whatsoever. She urged us to go ahead with the project, if we could get financing at a reasonable rate. However, she did warn us of the costs of the equipment we would need. We should've listened to her more intently.

Finding an appropriate building was easy enough, but finding medical equipment was a nightmare. The people who run medical equipment businesses should have opened up a college and taught people how to be crooks and thieves. But, if you needed the equipment, there's not a lot you could do except "bite the bullet" and give into these highway robbers. We started searching the networks for graduating doctors and found the market was a lot tighter than we anticipated. The doctors available wanted way more than we wanted to pay. Everybody wants to get rich.

Almost by accident, Amanda happened to hear through a nurse friend of hers about a medical school in Costa Rica that was sanctioned by the U.S. It was being used by students who couldn't afford the over-priced medical schools in America. It was relatively cheap for students and somewhat easy to get into, but upon graduation, it was very hard to get a job with a degree from Costa Rica. Most of the graduating doctors found work on cruise ships as ship doctors, with the Red Cross and other non-profits, or in third world countries. Very few were fortunate enough to find jobs in the United States. Two of the lucky ones were contacted by us and jumped at the opportunity to come aboard our fledgling clinic.

One of the newly graduated doctors, Tim, literally had all his clothes in one suitcase when he came to us. I had to help him with expenses because the poor guy had absolutely nothing. Tim grew up on the wrong side of Oakland, California. It was not a Golden State for him. His father abandoned him and his three siblings, and his mother worked as a waitress at an all night diner. His other siblings never graduated from high school and two of them ended up in gangs, while his only sister died from a drug overdose at 19 years of age. How Tim overcame this is truly heroic. How he then worked his way through the local city college and got accepted to medical school in Costa Rica is nothing short of miraculous.

Tim told me that when he was accepted into medical school in Costa Rica, he had no money and no transportation, and no idea how he'd even get to Costa

Rica. He had a part-time girlfriend who gave him $100 to help get him there, but airplane tickets were completely out of the question. Train and bus tickets were also too much, so Tim decided he'd start hitchhiking down the coast from Oakland towards Mexico.

He'd stop at any food banks, or Salvation Army's he could find on the way to sleep or maybe get a free meal. This worked pretty well until he got to Mexico. He said, in Mexico, the people there thought he was a rich American and it was hard getting across the country. He told me he slept many nights by just wandering off the side of the road and lying down among some trees or bushes.

On through Guatamala, Honduras and Nicaragua, he hitched rides on buses, flat bed trucks, semis, even once on a horse and buggy for a few miles. His money had long run out and he looked in the fields for anything he could eat. Fortunately for him crops were coming in and he found cucumbers, tomatoes, cantaloupes, and other types of vegetables he couldn't recognize. However, as he said, when you're starving, you're not really that picky. He finally made it to Costa Rica only to find that the medical school required a deposit from all students to get started. He had nothing.

He decided he'd hitchhike over to the coast and look for work to get the deposit money. He found a job in a local casino as a dishwasher. He washed dishes, he mopped floors, he cleaned the restrooms and he slept in a shack on the beach (which was a storage unit for umbrellas in the daytime). He ate leftovers off the plates coming back to the kitchen and he saved every penny he made until he had enough for the initial tuition to enter school.

When Tim finally enrolled in school, he immediately began worrying how he was going to pay for the next semester, since it took all he had for the current tuition. He knew being in medical school meant long hours of studying and work at the local hospital. What he didn't know was how he would be able to find a part-time job and still find time to sleep a couple of hours each night.

This is when fate entered Tim's life. Before class one morning he was sitting in an outdoor café reading a local newspaper someone had left behind, looking at the want ads for some type of job. The waitress, a local Costa Rican girl with long dark hair and beautiful eyes, came by and asked if he wanted coffee. He declined (since he had no money) and offered to leave the table for another paying customer.

She said, "Stay, it's okay, we're not that busy right now." Tim said a few minutes later, the same waitress brought him a cup of coffee and a sweet roll, telling him "a friend" had paid for it. Tim looked around and didn't notice anyone he knew, or didn't see anyone looking at him—but he was thankful for the roll and coffee. Next day, he went back to the same place, hoping his "friend" would be there again. Once again, he got a coffee and sweet roll, but still had no idea who this so-called "friend" was.

Tim, being the sort of person he was, felt he could not accept this charity any longer and determined he had to find out who this benefactor was and how he could repay this person. So, the next day, Tim told the waitress he would not accept any more free coffee or rolls unless he could meet the man responsible for this kindness. She told him that was impossible, since it wasn't a man. It was her. Tim was stunned and embarrassed to know that this lowly waitress was buying him food everyday with nothing expected in return.

When he regained his composure, he thanked her for her uncompromising kindness, but told her he could not take advantage of her any longer. She said "Do not worry senor. My father, who owns this café, is fully aware of what I'm doing and only wishes to see me happy." Tim said, "And buying me coffee and a sweet roll makes you happy?" That exchange led to a budding romance that still continues (albeit, long distance) today.

Tim is again saving his money, now for the purpose of being able to have a home so he can bring his fiancé from Costa Rica here to marry him. And, he's also saving so he can repay her father for paying his tuition for the remainder of his time in medical school.

Tim was an inspiration to talk to and I greatly admired his fortitude, resiliency and passion to obtain what he wanted. Which was a career and, more than a career, a wife to share his life with. Mostly, I was grateful to be able to employ a good man who had

143

worked so hard to fulfill his dream. I was very glad to have him.

———————

The other new doctor, Gabriel, had hair halfway down his back and wore round "granny glasses." But had the kind of caring personality that made you instantly trust him. Gabriel came from Kansas City, Missouri, from an average background and an average education. After college at the University of Missouri /Kansas City, he decided he wanted to be a professional musician. He played in bands throughout his high school and college years and according to him, could play a slide guitar nearly as well as Duane Allman. That's yet to be proven. He was always in demand to play and finally chose to join an up-and-coming band from Kansas City, Casey and the Sloopers. They had been looking for a guitar player to take on the road for extended tour dates their promoter had lined up.

What Gabriel didn't know was that the tour promoter was also a thief. When they finished their nearly eight months on the road, they not only did not make any money, but the band owed several companies quite a bit of money for transportation, lodging, food, etc. Their so-called "promoter" vanished with all their money and was nowhere to be found. This left a bad taste for the music business in Gabriel's life. No money, no career, nothing left but a desire to help people. Long story cut short, he applied to medical school in Costa Rica, got accepted, and here he is.

We were happy with our selections, but to cover ourselves, we made them sign five year contracts so they couldn't leave us empty handed if someone offered them a better opportunity. We were ready. Amanda recommended a couple of young nurses who were low on the totem pole at the hospital who were looking for something better. Then we found a P.A. from the local help wanted ads in the newspaper. We were now staffed, ready to go and totally unaware of what we were getting ourselves into.

From the day we opened the doors, we were besieged by the underprivileged, all looking for medical help. Almost all of them were unable to pay. But nearly all had some sort of medical card or government assurance that would ensure they received the help they needed. Our poor doctors, P.A. and nurses worked their tails off. Sixty to eighty hour work weeks became the norm, and we quickly had to add staff or lose the ones we had from burn out.

Instead of hiring another doctor or two, we went the cheaper route and hired two additional Physician Assistants. Truth be known, I think these P.A.'s knew almost as much as the doctors did. We hired two more nurses, recommended by Amanda. I wish we could've hired Amanda, but she made entirely too much money now and had become a nurse supervisor—which she loved.

I personally hired our office manager/ insurance expert. The only way we were going to make this thing work was by playing the insurance game and making sure we got paid from whatever agency, company or government that had the money. We needed someone sharp. We needed someone who knew how to play the game, someone who didn't mind cutting corners here and there. In short, someone like me.

I interviewed for two weeks. At least 15-20 people came into my office trying to sell themselves and convince me they knew everything about the insurance game. I'm sure they all did, but that's not what I was looking for. I was searching for that intangible quality, the self assurance and the confidence that told me this person would do whatever it took to be successful and to get the most out of our resources that was possible. How do you put that in an ad? You don't. You have to talk to people and listen to them and get a feel for them and wait until something clicks in you. When it does, you'll know. I knew within five minutes of my interview with Pam Woods that she was the person I was looking for.

Of the 20 or so applicants, Pam was the only female I interviewed. She immediately started saying "We need to do this", and "We need to do that", and more importantly, "If we really want to take advantage of all situations, then we need to..." Yes, Pam, we do want to take advantage of all situations. How do we do that, and when can you start?

Pam was the kind of woman you didn't question. She had a certain quality that made you implicitly believe her and trust her. Even though she was an attractive woman (full-bodied), when she told you something, you had to resist the urge to say "Yes sir." Pam was a single woman with no children, who moved here years ago with a deadbeat husband. She quickly dumped him when he wouldn't work. She's been single now for over fifteen years. And even though there have been many rumors of men (and women), no one here has ever seen her with anyone else, nor heard her mention anyone else. And, no one here, including me, is brave enough to ask her about it.

Pam had extensive experience in the medical insurance industry, even working for a short time with the Social Security Administration. That job didn't pay well enough, so she went back to the large insurance companies. She felt overlooked and underappreciated working for the large corporations. She was looking for a place where she could make a difference and be rewarded for hard work and innovation. Well Pam, I'm going to give you that chance. Prove me right.

Pam immediately started filing insurance claims and cutting through reams of red tape to ensure our payments were expedited, which was vital to a new organization which hadn't yet established a financial foothold. Soon, we had a positive cash flow, even with the burdening debt of all the medical equipment we had to buy. And one thing we could be absolutely certain of was that we would never run out of patients.

Our office stayed packed from opening time, till closing time, when we had to turn people away. Every once in a while we had patients who had insurance from their employers. Sometimes we even had cash paying customers. However, the overwhelming majority of our patients were on some sort of local, state or federal assistance that helped with medical costs.

My two partners made it clear they didn't have time to devote any of their schedules to helping with the clinic. They basically just came up with the idea and helped arrange some of the financing.

They made sure they had their names on all partnership documents and then sat back to receive any profits we would get. I really didn't mind being the decision-maker on most issues, I trusted me more than them anyway. But, I still had my own business to run, and I wasn't a doctor. So I let Pam and the doctors basically run the business. They knew what they were doing. They'd just let me know if they needed something and how things were generally going.

We had to replace one of the nurses after the first month. She simply couldn't cope with the non-stop activity and volume of patients that were coming through our clinic. However, I kept a keen eye on the financial aspects of the business. We had invested a lot of money on this and even though I felt really good about it, I was still going to keep a close eye on everything involving money, payments and invoices. I knew there were a lot of people out there just like me.

19

Amanda had been feeling a little under the weather for several days. She just couldn't seem to shake whatever little bug she'd caught. This went on for a few weeks when I finally insisted she see a doctor. When she finally did get a checkup, they found a small tumor in her intestines. When you hear something like that, your whole world goes blank and it scares you to death. Amanda had tests done and a biopsy. We were told it would be a few days before the results came back. Those were the longest three days in the history of mankind.

Of course, she acted like nothing was wrong and went to work all three days. I tried to work each day, but, I couldn't concentrate on anything. So I ended up at the lake, with my fishing pole. All three days I was begging God to heal Amanda, trying to make a deal with Him if He'd heal Amanda, I would change FOREVER! I'd be a new man. I'd go to church regularly. I'd be someone He would be proud of. Well, God kept His end of the bargain, the tumor was benign and Amanda was fine. I kept my promises for about seven days—maybe eight. Does He actually remember everything we promise? Does forgiveness cover stuff like this? I need to do a lot more fishing.

Once money started coming into the clinic regularly and we could somewhat plan for the future, we hired another doctor who spoke Spanish fluently. Again, the doctor was from the same school in Costa Rica that the other two had come from. Rodolfo, or Rudy as we all called him, was your stereotypical Latin Don Juan. Roman features, moderately long flowing hair, which he swooped back, glistening white teeth, and just enough of an accent to drive the women crazy. However, he was as gay as they come.

He told us up front in the interview about his sexual orientation.

All we were concerned with was that he knew what he was doing. That he would be able to get along with Tim and Gabriel (the other two doctors). And, that he was willing to accept our pay offer and would sign the five year agreement. He did. I'm pretty sure all the staff knew about Rudy, and it was never an issue as far as I know. His looks probably helped bring in some female patients, hoping to latch onto this handsome, foreign doctor. Good luck with that.

Unlike Tim and Gabriel, Rudy came from a wealthy family in Colombia. He never mentioned how his family came into their money and we didn't ask. We do know they weren't into farming or industry or tourism—so, you do the math. Gabriel ended up in medical school in Costa Rica because his father thought it was the best thing to do under the circumstances. According to Rudy, those circumstances being that his father caught him and his boyfriend at the lake house in a very compromising situation.

Rudy just seemed happy to be in the United States. He was a great doctor, very caring and apparently had no money concerns. He drove a BMW and bought (I mean paid in cash), a new condo in the downtown area. I found out later that Rudy also helped Tim with a "loan" to help bring his fiancé to America so they could marry. He was a good guy and a great doctor.

Soon, we added another P.A. and two more nurses assistants, along with some office staff to handle the mountains of paperwork it took to process all the claims. Pam oversaw all insurance claims and nothing left our office unless she personally approved it. It also became apparent we were running out of space. Instead of moving everything into a new building, we decided to simply knock out a wall and expand into the parking lot. Nearly as soon as the renovation was complete, it seemed we were out of room again.

Apparently there was no end to the number of people seeking medical help.

Every week or so, I would come over and take Pam out to a long lunch. We would discuss the business, what was happening at the clinic, what needed to happen and how we could grow things. She was a very perceptive woman and also someone who looked at everything. By this I mean, how things worked. Why other things didn't work. How the whole system of claims, payments, records of payments, and checks and balances connected—everything.

After a dozen or so of these working lunches with Pam, where I became more and more comfortable with her, I began to ask shaded questions. Like, "Is there any way to increase our net income from the insurance payments?" "Is one agency better than another at processing and paying?" "How closely do they monitor their patients and the claims?" "Do they have processes in place to ensure they are indeed paying out correctly and not over-paying or underpaying?" The deviousness in me wanted to know how these things worked. Were there any opportunities for us to take advantage of any loopholes anywhere? Did the whole insurance system monitor itself to ensure everything happened as it should happen?

The answer to this was exactly what I thought it would be. The entire insurance conglomerate was so big and so disjointed that one hand truly had no clue what the other hand was doing. In fact, on closer inspection, I wondered how in the world they got anything done. It became perfectly apparent that the whole industry was totally incompetent. The people processing claims were mostly high school graduates making little more than minimum wage. The managers in charge (if you can make that inference), were over- worked, under-paid and past the point of really caring what actually happened, as long as no one above them complained.

Soon, my questions to Pam became more pointed and more direct. She understood exactly where I was going and started giving me answers to questions I hadn't even asked. Working mostly with the Hispanic population, as we did, we had multiple patients named Jose Martinez, or Ana Gomez, or Pedro Fernandez... many patients with the same names. I asked how the insurance companies or agencies knew if they had paid the claim for the "right" Jose Martinez and not the "wrong" Jose Martinez? The answer Pam gave me floored me. They had no clue!

Whether it was the sick Jose or the other non-sick Jose, when we filed a claim, they paid it. Furthermore, sometimes, our clerks inadvertently filed Jose's claim with two agencies, instead of just one. And both agencies paid! Of course, Pam returned one of the checks to the unwitting agency. The sad part of this deal was that it was almost impossible to return a double check. First, they couldn't believe a mistake had been made and second, no one seemed to know how to cancel the payment and debit the organization who wrote the check. It seemed it was way more trouble for them to cancel the duplicate check than it was to just let it go.

I could help with that.

Quickly, Pam and I were on the same page. Any double payments were not to be returned. And if a "mistake" was made by us, by double billing or billing for the wrong "Jose", well, if they caught our mistake, then we would apologize and reimburse them. Guess what? For the next six months, they never caught anything. We were never questioned about anything, and kept sending us checks as fast as they could process them. Things just started growing from there. Soon we were double-billing nearly every Hispanic patient, and no one at any of these insurance conglomerates had a clue, nor cared, what was happening. If someone at some behemoth of an agency would have ever questioned anything, we would simply have apologized for the oversight and returned the duplicate billing. That never happened.

This was a little dangerous for me, trusting someone else with one of my schemes. However, once Pam was in, who would she tell without implicating herself? Plus, I trusted her. Obviously, she didn't get involved with this because she liked me. She loved the extra money she was getting. Pam would get a nice percentage of the proceeds from all double billings. And she would shield those profits from anyone else, including my two so-called partners, who were oblivious to the whole scheme. I set aside a special account in a new bank to deposit these double payments. An account no one knew existed but me and Pam. Even Amanda didn't know.

A couple of years into the clinic business, I decided to buy the company from my two partners. I did not want them prying too much into the records of our clinic, especially with their accountants. The clinic was doing okay on its own. Of course, my two partners had no idea how well I was really doing. I made them a financial offer they couldn't refuse and, the deal was done quickly. I was now the sole owner of my little money-making clinic. I don't know if my guilt or conscience or what overcame me, but I volunteered to start a Saturday morning free, walk-in clinic for children only.

No prescriptions would be written. It only had a P.A. and a nurse helper. That was all, we only saw children, no adults. Many of the families offered to pay something ($5, $10, etc. or even pay in food), but we would take no payment from them. We just wanted the children to get better. Don't misunderstand me. Again, I'm not justifying what we did was okay because we gave free medical care to some kids. Not at all. However, sometimes, even the worst of us seem to have a heart. Don't believe everything you think.

The clinic ran well for years. We kept adding staff and increasing services. But, as much as I tried to stay out of the day-to-business, I was always needed to do something, buy something or settle some disagreement. I liked the money I was earning, but it was starting to irritate me a little and take up way more time than I wanted to devote to it. Honestly, I had done better financially than I ever thought I would—ever dreamed I would! In fact, I was now

155

beginning to have money problems. I didn't need more money. I had too much money that was unaccounted for. Specifically, all the cash I'd been accumulating for years from my business. And the cash from my "investments" with Mike which was all sitting in safe deposit boxes around town.

Thinking about all this money and how I'd obtained it resulted in my fishing trips not being as much fun as they used to be. I knew the answers now before I asked the questions. I also knew God had to be unhappy with all my dealings. He had to be. I used every conceivable rationalization I could think of; every "cock-eyed" justification there was. But none of them worked. "Wasn't it enough that I was a good, solid husband, who loved his wife and treated her like the princess she was? Or that I loved and cared for my parents and Amanda's parents as well? Or that I..." No George, it's not!

I seriously thought of baiting a hook now and actually trying to catch a fish. Anything to silence the thoughts and voices in my mind. But, I didn't.

Now, back to my full-time job—keeping Amanda happy. I knew she had been exploring options for us. I told her to plan anything she wanted. Wherever she wanted to go was fine with me. Here's why I'll never figure out this amazing woman. She was given free reign to plan our vacation anywhere in the world, and she chose Washington, DC, less than a hundred miles from our house. However, we did stay in an upscale lodge in Georgetown—very pricy and very elegant— Amanda loved it. We toured the White House, but really didn't have time to meet the President. We were on a tight schedule.

We visited the Lincoln Memorial, and stared up at the great man.

We visited the Jefferson Memorial, where we learned that Thomas Jefferson never had a dinner with anyone in his life that he felt was his intellectual equal. The possible exception was when he once dined alone during a snowstorm. We climbed to the top of the Washington Monument and walked solemnly around the Vietnam War Memorial. Washington is indeed a tourist's goldmine. We loved it.

We saved the best for last...The Smithsonian.

We spent almost two and a half days at the various Smithsonian museums—all fascinating! We saw a fossil they claimed was over 3.5 billion years old (How do they know that?) We saw the Apollo lunar landing module and the ruby slippers that Judy Garland wore in the Wizard of Oz. We saw shrunken heads (from some unfortunate humans), dinosaur poop, gallstones from President Grover Cleveland, the world's longest beard (18 ½ feet), which was cut off a Norwegian man when he died, and locks of hair from the first 14 U.S. Presidents. All of this was fascinating, if not a little bizarre. Only one exhibit got to me emotionally. It was the display case containing the suit and tie President Kennedy was wearing when he was shot. The bullet holes were clearly visible and the memories never forgotten.

I had around a dozen safe deposit boxes full of cash, mostly hundred dollar bills, stashed at various banks around town now. No one knew about these but me. Nice problem to have right? But, it's really hard to use that money, I can't deposit it in my accounts at the bank. If so, it would raise too many eyebrows. I can't invest cash money in the stock market or any real estate deals. I was glad to have it, but I didn't really know what to do with it. I'll have to figure that out later.

My regular accounts were hefty on their own. I had my regular business, which was still booming. I had the proceeds from the clinic, plus all the double payments in a separate account. I was making money from Amanda's dad's stock dividends every quarter, plus my own investments were doing very well. I was well over a millionaire, not even counting all the cash I had stashed away. Apparently, I was on top of the world.

Then, just when you feel invincible, when you're living the dream, king of your own little kingdom, something always happens to bring you back to reality. With me, it was Pam Woods. Pam was virtually running the clinic now, not the medical side, but everything else. We'd decided to stop the double-billing with most patients. We didn't want to become too greedy. I guess we assumed a little greed was okay.

She was just doing it enough for me and her to significantly pad our accounts and keep them growing.

Plus, we simply did not feel that bad about it, since we were only double-billing government agencies. And, doesn't everyone enjoying screwing the government as much as possible? We did. Pam and I would still meet every week for lunch and review the business, just talk about things and catch up basically. She seemed to really enjoy these meetings and they started lasting longer and longer. I didn't really mind, Pam was fun to talk to and always had ideas on how to better things.

Almost imperceptively, the chemistry started changing between us. I can't really pinpoint any one time or any specific event, but things changed. And not the way I wanted them to change. As I said earlier, Pam was an attractive woman, once you got past the businesswoman part of her. First, I noticed that she started dressing differently for our lunches...I'd NEVER seen her with more than one button open on her blouses before. Now, two or sometimes three were left unbuttoned.

Pam nearly always wore pant suits to work. But now for our lunches she was wearing dresses, sometimes dresses that were provocatively short for someone her age and stature. Of course, I noticed these changes, it was hard not to. As I said, she was an attractive woman. I figured she'd met a man (or woman) and was dressing for that particular person. I was still woefully oblivious to anything personal between us and went weeks not suspecting anything out of the ordinary. That is, until we met one day at a new restaurant, one with dim lighting (even at noon). When I arrived, Pam was at a corner table at the back

159

of the restaurant waiting on me, still nothing really out of place.

She had some files she wanted me to look over after we'd eaten. We were sitting in a corner booth and after we finished, she sort of slid around close to me to show me the files. Her leg brushed against mine, but I'm still deaf, dumb and happy. I did notice her blouse was unbuttoned a little more than usual and quite a bit of cleavage was appearing on the scene. Hmm. As I tried not to look (unsuccessfully), she leaned over to show me some numbers, put her hand on my hand and her left boob pressed against my right elbow. Okay! Now I get it!

Very awkwardly, I slid away, saying the files all looked good to me. Then I told her I really needed to get back to the office. I didn't know what else to say, this is something I never envisioned happening— EVER. After I got back to work, I started thinking about the whole thing. Maybe my imagination just went overboard. I probably overreacted a bit; I'm really quite sure Pam never meant anything at all. Yep, that's it George, you just overreacted—you big, dumb jerk. I hope I didn't embarrass her. Then, as I was starting to feel a little better, my personal phone rang—the number only Pam, Amanda and my mom called me on. I looked at the caller ID and it wasn't Amanda or my mom calling.

"Hello?" Please Lord, let this call be about business.

Please! No, it was Pam. She told me she wanted us to take our relationship to the next level. I said, "Pam, there is no next level. There's not even a previous level, or a current level. I'm sorry if I did something to mislead you, but I'm the happiest married man in the world. It has nothing to do with you, but Amanda means the whole world to me." She said "Okay, I understand." And she hung up the phone.

Oh my God, what am I going to do now? Certainly, the lunches will end, no doubt about that. I started wondering if she would do anything, or say anything to anyone about our business with the double-billings? Women can be spiteful when scorned. Did I scorn her? That sounds like an 18th century term. I did something to her and I don't feel good about this, not good at all.

The next week, we obviously did not meet for lunch. I also noticed that our special account for the double-billings did not have any credits for the week. The next week, same thing—no credits. Next week—no credits. Okay...I'll call now. This was not an easy call to make. She answered and I asked her about the credits for the account. She said she thought we ought to stop what we're doing and disperse the account. What could I say? Without her, I couldn't do anything. So I said "Fine, I'll send you your share and close the account immediately." She didn't even say "Thank you" before she hung up.

I closed the account the next day. Then I went to one of my safe deposit boxes and took out enough cash, in hundred dollar bills, for Pam's share. I put the money in a travel bag and took it to the clinic, went to her office, dropped it on the floor and walked out, vowing to never set foot in there again.

I shouldn't have let my emotions alter my decision-making so drastically, but I simply wanted to be away from her for several different reasons now. One of the big medical conglomerates had made several overtures in the past about wanting to "merge" our now not-so-little clinic with their operations. I called them and asked if they wanted to buy me out— they jumped at the chance. Before the dust settled, I was counting the money from the sale and extremely relieved to be shed of that headache. Will I miss my little clinic? Undoubtedly. I birthed it and nursed to adulthood; I was proud of it. And, it made me a whole lot of money. So, one headache gone. "Congratulations George...you did the right thing."

Aw shut up!

Well, whether I wanted it or not, I now had free time on my hands. There were several ideas I had brewing, but nothing concrete, just some thoughts, the main one being to continue keeping Amanda happy. For years now she had been urging me to plan a grand vacation for us, something memorable, magical and wonderful. Now, I was ready. The clinic was gone, my other business was smooth, I was getting rich quickly and I loved where I was in my life. Whereas I am what I am; Amanda is beyond belief. Apparently, she gets more beautiful every year. If she ever gets a wrinkle, it's a beauty wrinkle...age is definitely making her better.

We've always taken some time off here and there...fancy resorts in Miami or New York... seemingly the same old things each year. She now wanted an adventure, something we would always remember, and by gosh, I was going to give her one. Unlike me, Amanda kept herself in shape by exercising, doing Yoga and Pilates and eating healthy. I wasn't in bad shape, but I certainly wasn't in good shape either. But now, I had to go on a 4-week cardio enhanced program so that I could give Amanda what she wanted. A three week guided hike along the Pacific

Crest Trail in the mountainous, wilderness areas of California!

When she first told me what she wanted, I thought she was joking, I really did. Heck, we'd never camped out before. The closest we'd ever come to that was spending the night in a Motel 6 in Norfolk. Now, three weeks in the wilderness? Camping? Hiking?

The things we do for love. We would have a guide with us (an expensive guide I might add). Other than that, we'd carry our sleeping bags, food and whatever else we needed on our backs. This is why I had to commit to an accelerated cardio program to get ready for this ordeal. I think you and I both know four weeks was not enough time. However, if Amanda wanted it, I would give it to her, or die trying—which seemed the likely result of this adventure for me.

Amanda convinced me to join Fitness World, a local gym, and hire a personal trainer to help me "get in shape". My first day in the gym was really eye-opening. More spandex in that one building than the rest of the city combined. There were groups of people who apparently did not mix with other groups of people—segregation in the truest form—not racially, but physically. First, men did not mix with women, the groups were separate. Next, the brutes and steroid junkies kept to themselves at the back of the gym grunting and screaming with every rep they did. I'm not sure if that was to impress everyone else, or to impress themselves.

Then, you had the women who dominated the cardio equipment—the elliptical machines, treadmills, bicycles and stair climbers. Finally, all the other men (who didn't have big muscles but wanted big muscles) worked out on all the various other machines. While discretely eyeing the corner where the brutes were, silently convincing themselves that they too could one day enter that corner of high voltage, bulging-muscles manhood.

I did not fit in at Fitness World. I wore my old grass stained tennis shoes that I mowed the lawn with, my aqua-colored Bermuda shorts and a tee-shirt that read "Make love, not war." Since our country was not presently at war with anyone, I'm quite certain this missive from the 60's was well over everyone's collective head.

However, my personal trainer, Jerry, was extremely happy to see me—like, abnormally happy. Jerry had glistening white teeth, $180 gym shoes, spandex shorts (which really made me question Jerry's sexuality) and a form-fitting muscle shirt that read "Personal Trainer," so I would be able to identify him in a crowd.

Jerry sized me up and decided to work on my "delts and lats" first...No Jerry! Whatever delts and lats are, mine are fine. I only wanted to work on whatever would get me through three weeks in the wilderness without dying. Well, Jerry seemed disappointed, but he didn't want to lose his $25 per thirty minute fee, so he quickly came up with a new plan.

As we walked over to the Stairmaster, an attractive, middle- aged woman, completely soaked in perspiration, with 0% body fat, was just getting off the machine and gathering her stuff up. She had an empty bottle of energy drink, a book about Early American Art, an ipod, a towel, and a yellow magic marker—which I found totally weird. She looked at me and said, "Let me wipe it down for you." My mind went completely in the gutter imagining what she meant, until she got a paper towel and wiped off the handles to the Stairmaster.

Jerry told me to "climb aboard," so I did. I grabbed my bottle of sweet tea and stepped onto the monster. The control panel looked like the dash of a 747. It had so many buttons and dials I didn't know where to start. Jerry quickly set the controls for me and there I went. Climbing, stepping, huffing, puffing, aching, with my legs burning and Jerry urging me onward. I took a quick sip of sweet tea for energy and keep going until I absolutely could not take another breath. I hit the stop button while I gasped for air and tried not to faint. When the torture machine stopped, I looked down at the dials and saw that I'd burned 73 calories in my 4 minutes and 37 seconds aboard. Jerry didn't look very impressed. But I was still alive, and that's all I cared about.

Somehow, I made it through the entire session with Jerry.

However, his over-zealoused urging, white-toothed smile personality combined with my aching, tormented body insured this would be my first and last session with a personal trainer. I didn't need this crap to walk through the mountains. I'll be fine. Of course, I didn't tell Amanda that I'd stopped my personal training. She thought I was still going to my sessions three times each week. It's a good thing Krispy Kreme isn't located on the route Amanda takes to the hospital. That would be hard to explain to her. I'll be fine.

Amanda started planning for our trip. She bought us backpacks, sleeping bags, mats, bug spray, flashlights, new hiking boots, all sorts of energy bars and protein junk. Whatever she wanted and whatever she did was fine with me—as long as she was happy. The last week before we left, she was so excited I'm not sure she ever slept. She packed and re-packed our gear, we tried everything on (the backpacks were a tad heavy, but we'd get used to them, wouldn't we?).

We'd never been gone for anywhere near three weeks before, there was a lot to do. I was a little concerned about my business, I'd have to trust things would be okay. However, I would still worry about it. The night before we left, she said we could "splurge" and eat whatever we wanted, especially since I'd been so good about completing my training. When in fact, I didn't need any help from a trainer eating doughnuts, especially the hot ones.

We were so tired from packing and getting everything ready that we just ordered a pizza, and it was delicious. But I had bad dreams that night, not scary stuff, just bad stuff, fueled by too much pepperoni and a great apprehension of "Can I do this?" Too late now George. You should've thought about this four weeks ago and spent your time with Jerry, instead of riding around the block at Krispy Kreme waiting for the red light to come on. Idiot!

We flew out early the next morning, I was glad to wake up from a night of dreadfulness. After the long cross-country flight and gathering up all our gear, we started out. Amanda was so excited she couldn't sit still or stop talking. I wasn't. We drove up to meet our guide, a young bearded guy named Seth, at Sequoia National Park, which is near Mt. Whitney. Seth was a professional guide in the spring and summer and a ski instructor in the winter. He told us he'd take care of everything and assured us we'd be fine. Little did he know of my glazed doughnut training regimen.

Seth grew up in a commune in northern California, and had lived the nomadic, hippie lifestyle we'd only read about before. His parents were true flower children and raised Seth and three siblings in a communal setting. They raised their own food and lived off the land as much as possible, an idyllic existence. However, he said they were hungry all the time, broke all the time, overworked and unhappy nearly all his childhood. His parents finally gave it all up when the kids were older, moved to Carmel and opened a Bed-and- Breakfast, which has done very well according to Seth.

That evening Seth inspected our gear and took out nearly half of what we had packed. This really hurt Amanda's feelings. We would later thank Seth for his experience and common sense. We would only carry enough food to last several days, whereupon Seth would then hike out by himself to nearby stores or villages and bring back more food. It was senseless for us to try and carry everything on our backs for the whole trip. He took away our flashlights, bug spray, some of our extra clothing, soap, utensils and urged us not to bring any books or my journal. Too bad, I was taking my journal to record this death march.

We started out that spring morning from Sequoia National Park, headed north along the trail through the mountains towards Kings Canyon National park. Springtime in the mountains can bring big temperature changes throughout the day and night. It can be crisp early in the morning, heat up during the day and be downright cold at night. We had to bring clothes for all these scenarios. Half way through the first day, my shoulders were aching from carrying the backpack and my feet were hurting from my new, unbroken-in hiking boots. At camp that night, my journal went into the campfire as well and as any other item I could think of that would lessen the load I had to carry.

I easily remembered why I didn't like camping. Let me list a few of the reasons: you have to sleep on the ground—it's hard. There are no bathrooms, and you must carry out all waste material (like toilet paper—think about that). There are no showers, you get dirty quickly—and stay that way. Did I mention that you have to sleep on the rock-hard ground? These little nuisances didn't seem to bother Amanda very much. They bothered me a lot, but I would not—I

WOULD NOT· complain and ruin her fantasy vacation.

I should've brought more Advil. I should've brought less of everything else. I should've stayed home. My shoulders hurt, my back hurt, my legs ached and my feet were blistered. We got a day of rest at King's Canyon, but it wasn't enough. Amanda, being a nurse, was concerned about my blistered feet, that they might become infected. I lied to her and told they were fine, I felt great! Up a mountain, across a trail, eat bland food, poop in the woods, sand in your toothpaste, sand in your food, sand up your nose...but if it made Amanda happy, I'd do it till I died. Oh Lord, please don't let me die out here.

Day after day we walked. Seth brought me back some Aleve from one of his side trips because he could tell I was in so much pain. The scenery was awesome, but it just wasn't worth it for me. Nothing was worth the misery I was in. A little over halfway into the death march, we came to another resting place where we would spend one night at the Vermillion Valley Resort. We could actually get a room here, have a hot meal, shower and sleep in a bed—SLEEP IN A BED! My poor feet were a bloody mess. I was addicted to Advil and Aleve. I hated my backpack, and thought of deserting. A firing squad would be okay at this point. But, how could I disappoint Amanda? I couldn't. I'd endure. I'd march on. I'd die before I disappointed her.

We woke from our amazingly soft bed the next morning and started gathering up our stuff. Amanda took an unusually long shower, and when she came out, she sat on the bed and said, "Honey, this isn't as much fun as I thought it would be. Would you hate me too much if I said I'd like to go home now?" "Baby", I said, "if you want to go home, we'll go...whatever will make you happy." It was all I could do not to turn flips and dance a jig in that hotel room. I acted sad on the outside and was bursting with joy on the inside.

I told Seth we were leaving. He was fine, especially when I paid him in full for the whole trip, plus gave him a nice tip. We arranged transportation back to our rental car, made our way to Los Angeles and booked a room at a resort overlooking the Pacific. We stayed there and healed, somewhat. We had room service, we had drinks (with ice), we had a soft bed, and we had each other. That was all that really mattered. On the way to the airport, we saw some homeless people. We stopped and gave them our sleeping bags and backpacks. They were thrilled to get them, we were happy to get rid of them. Let's go home.

I thought of that trip for many years afterwards. Though we never truly discussed it, I'm almost certain Amanda stopped the trip when she did only for me. Though I never complained, she could see the pain I was in. She knew; she stopped for me. That's the way she was.

I loved our home. I loved being back home. Everything was fine at work. Mom was great. My brother Teddy had met some older woman and moved in with her. And Frankie was living in a pay-by- the- week apartment. One of the doctors from clinic, Rudy, called me and said the new owners of my old clinic started changing everything. Pam had a bad disagreement with them and quit and now he was going to leave the clinic to start a practice of his own, specifically catering to the AIDS population.

He asked me if I wanted to help him and Pam start up the new place. It sounded exciting and I really liked Rudy, but I knew I could never work with Pam again. I thought long and hard about it, but in the end, I just didn't want to get involved with Pam or in the medical field again. Maybe I was getting too old, or maybe too rich already, I don't know, but I just didn't want to go through that again. I helped him arrange some financing, pointed him in the right direction, but otherwise, I stayed out.

Rudy and Pam tried as hard as they could to make their AIDS clinic a success, but it never got off the ground. It seems that AIDS patients don't have the insurance coverage, or the governmental support that legal and illegal immigrants have. Although there were plenty of patients who needed help, there just wasn't enough funding to keep the clinic operative.

Rudy ended up moving to Asheville, N.C. and working in the local hospital there. He keeps in touch with me occasionally and seems to be very happy now that he's met his life's partner high up there in the Blue Ridge Mountains. Pam disappeared, at least from my life and our community. No one has seen her or heard from her since the AIDS clinic closed. Rudy thinks she met someone from Washington, D.C. on the internet. He wasn't sure, and as always, she never volunteered any information. I hope she's happy, wherever she is.

Amanda was planning a three day weekend for us in the mountains. She called my mom to let her know we'd be away. They laughed and shared some stories, said their goodbyes and Amanda and I went out to dinner, came home, packed our stuff and went to bed. As I was in the shower the next morning, I heard Amanda scream. I jumped out of the shower, wet and dripping, looked at Amanda and she told me my mom had died. Mom went to sleep the night before and never woke up this morning. Just like that—my mother was gone.

We found out a heart attack had killed her in her sleep. They found her in the morning, on her side, her hands folded up under her chin, just like I'd seen her sleeping a hundred times before. It was hard. It was harder for my two brothers. They always had a security blanket with mom. The visitation, the funeral, and all the family stuff was very trying and tiring. Now, the really hard part came; explaining to Frankie and Teddy that they will get nothing from Mom's Will except $50 each.

I decided to let them hear the news from the lawyer as he read the will in front of us all in his office. As a precaution, I hired two guys (two big guys from my plant) to put on suits, act as lawyers and stand in the corner of the office as the Will was read. I had no idea how my brothers would react, or what they'd try to do. After the Will was read, they both got up, without looking at me or speaking to me and walked out. It seems mom had informed them of the Will's contents after they kept bugging her about wanting to borrow some more money against their part of the so-called inheritance. She finally told them what I'd done.

Between mom's and dad's life insurance policies, her savings and the money Mike had made them, Mom had quite a substantial portfolio. Amanda urged me to "share" some of this money with my brothers. "How could I?" I asked. "Look what they've done with their lives. If I give them any money, they'll just spend it on drink and drugs. It'll be like throwing Mom's money down the sewer." Amanda looked at me and said, "They're your Mom and Dad's children. They're your brothers, George. Give them some money.

Not much, but you give them some money." I did.

We settled on $5,000 each and then took bets with each other to see how long it would be before they came back wanting to "borrow" some more. I paid them in hundred dollar bills. They took the money, never said "Thank you" or "Screw you", and walked away. I haven't seen them since. I keep up with them, through sources, but I haven't seen them or heard from them since that day.

I was getting older now. People who knew me kept coming to me with deals and offers to make money. I kept turning them down. Why? I don't truly know. People don't change; I didn't change. I wasn't magically a good person now. But for some unknown reason, I wasn't interested in any deals. I did, however, enjoy fishing more and more, or the pretense of fishing. I really just wanted the time alone and the conversations with God. As time passed, I found the conversations became more and more one-sided. That is—He was talking to me a lot more than I was talking to Him. Before you think I'm crazy, NO, I did not actually hear any voices. But if you listen carefully enough, you can hear what you need to hear—even what you don't want to hear.

I started reading the Bible fairly regularly, mostly in my boat out on the lake where no one could see me. Many times I wished I had someone there to help explain things to me. Some ideas and concepts, I didn't understand. Other things I understood completely, but didn't, (or couldn't), accept the reality of them. One passage I read over and over and over, hoping for a revelation from above: "If we confess our sins, He is faithful and just to forgive us our sins and to cleanse us from all unrighteousness." I looked up towards heaven for inspiration, but all I saw were a few puffy white clouds and a buzzard soaring around in long, looping circles. Never once flapping his wings, just riding the thermals, looking down on all of us earthbound creatures, being glad he's who he is...and not one of us.

Since I now had all of my mother's money, I felt a responsibility to do something with it and put it to work. So I went to see a financial advisor, who referred me to an acquaintance of his in the investment field. I set up a meeting with Herman and we discussed all sorts of strategies—long term and short term. He was fascinating to talk with and opened my eyes to different opportunities I was unaware of.

Herman was a bit older than me and had been in the investment field for many years. In fact, he started as a trader on Wall Street, working directly on the floor. One of those guys you see on TV yelling and screaming to buy and sell. Herman now had his own business and from the looks of things, he was doing very well. I checked him out with several people and they all said the same thing..."You're going to love dealing with Herman."

But before I gave someone my money again, I was going to check them out personally. Herman went to Duke and then got an MBA from Brown University...okay, so far I'm impressed. He's been married to his college sweetheart since graduating.

She taught high school for a few years, but retired to raise their four children.

Herman has several holdings, as well as a home in an upscale neighborhood here, and an oceanfront home at Virginia Beach (and those aren't cheap). He's been in business here for over twenty years with a solid reputation. Okay Herman, I'm sold. How can you help me?

Herman was not your typical stockbroker. Most of those guys "advise" you to buy and sell so they can get commissions on all your trades. Really, whether you lose money or gain money is not the main objective with them. They are more concerned that you make trades—that's how they get paid. Herman didn't operate in that traditional manner. Herman was a bit like Mike, in that you had to trust him entirely. But Herman was above board and totally legitimate, whereas Mike was as shady as they come. I'm not complaining about Mike, I wish he was still in business. I'm only saying Mike definitely operated in the shadows.

If you invested with Herman, everything was done legally. You got receipts and documents and papers and forms and all sorts of regulations and signed statements. The kicker was, you authorized Herman to use your money for trades and trusted him to invest, and to buy and sell at his discretion. In essence, you were blindly trusting Herman with your money, with no guarantees of anything.

Every month, Herman's office would send me a statement telling me how much money was invested, how much was in escrow and how much my total investment had grown (or not) that month. It always grew. Herman's clients trusted him implicitly and never questioned what he was doing with their funds. As long as your monthly statements continued to grow and your money was insured, why question how old Herman was weaving his magic. Except that I was curious.

When something seems a little too good, there's usually a little "bad" mixed in there somewhere. But it didn't matter how many phone calls I made to Herman, how many lunches or dinners I had with him, even how I confided some "business secrets" to him. He still would never divulge any information to me about anything regarding his business. Dang!

Every month, positive growth, nothing eye-opening, but gains after gains after gains. Now, if you know anything about the stock market, you know full well that it doesn't go up EVERY month. There are periods of ups and downs and you try to make the best decisions you can and take the good while minimizing the bad. Only with Herman, there was never a bad month...ever. How was he doing this? Each month I became more and more intrigued to the point of becoming obsessed with trying to understand how Herman was doing what he was doing. "George, why can't you just leave well enough alone? Why can't you be normal? Why do you always have to be you?" I thought I had that little voice under control.

180

23

In my main business, we had a computer nerd who did virtually everything for us. Henry programmed the network, set up the system, monitored everything, kept viruses out, did all the repairs and maintained everyone's laptop or PC. Henry was a nice kid. You know his type—thick glasses, oddly matched clothes, bad complexion, trying to grow a mustache—but couldn't. He was a little overweight, shy and had absolutely NO personality. But he'd do whatever I wanted him to.

What I wanted him to do was way over his nerdy little head.

What I wanted was information. I know all these geek types network with each other and they all know who knows what. I wanted him to tell me how to contact the "geekiest of the geeks," the "nerdiest of the nerds", the guy who was so cutting edge that he could never expect to find a girlfriend his entire life!

"Oh", Henry said, "You want to meet Abbey." I said, "If this girl is the smartest one around, then yes, I do." "No" Henry told me, "Abbey is not a girl, he's from India. His name is Abhinandan, but he goes by

Abbey. He's in his last year at Virginia Tech, in the doctoral program for Computational Science and Engineering." Okay, great, if this is the chief nerd, then Abbey and I have a lot to discuss. Henry gave me Abbey's phone number, but warned me he was hard to catch, since he worked in the computer lab long hours and was seldom at his little dump of an apartment. That was music to my ears, "…dump of an apartment." Abbey just might be interested in making a little money on the side as my consultant.

Henry was right. I called Abbey's number probably twenty times before he finally answered. He certainly didn't sound Indian, I detected no accent whatsoever. He just sounded like any other computer junkie— normal. He told me he was very busy and didn't really have the time to meet me, even after I told him I was friends with Henry—"Who?" He said. "Your computer friend Henry Ellison" I replied. He had no idea who I was referring to. Obviously, Henry had exaggerated his so-called friendship with Abbey.

Abbey, however, did know who Benjamin Franklin was and what his picture was on—hundred dollar bills. I've always found that Ben can be quite the ice-breaker in awkward situations. We set up a meeting late Friday afternoon. Abbey said he couldn't meet long, he had an engagement he simply couldn't miss.

We met at a local bar that hadn't yet filled up with the after work crowd. Just the closet drinkers and alcoholics leaning against the bar, nursing their second, or third, or fourth Jim Beam, Jack Daniels, or Iron Maiden of the day. I figured Abbey wouldn't be that hard to spot. I was sure there wouldn't be too many nerdy, geeky Indian guys strolling in.

I was right. He wasn't hard to spot, but he was definitely not nerdy or geeky. Abbey looked like—I don't know a famous Indian celebrity to compare him to—he looked like a movie star, or, at least a reality show star. He was dressed in a form fitting suit, carrying an expensive brief case, with a picture perfect smile as he greeted me. I was a tad bit intimidated by his appearance.

He immediately said, "I don't have long, how can I help you?" So, without beating around the bush, I told him. I wanted to hack into the computer system of Herman's company—not to steal anything, not to copy anything, not to compromise anything. All I wanted was some information for my own personal knowledge. How was Herman doing his trading in order to make profits every single month? I just wanted to know—I HAD to know. Is this hacking even possible to do? And, could he do it? If so, how much would it cost me?

Abbey looked at me for about ten seconds, then asked "Are you the police?" "Of course not." I said. He then said "Meet me here tomorrow morning at 10:00 and bring $2500 in cash." "Whoa, I'm not paying you up front. I'll pay you when you get me the information." Abbey replied, "I'd have you the information in 10 minutes if it weren't for her." He pointed towards the door where the most beautiful, blonde, long-legged creature you've ever seen was just walking in. He said, "I can't keep my date waiting. If you want the information, be here in the morning at

10:00." Wow...I mean double Wow; first to the girl, then, was it that easy? I'd find out in the morning.

I was at the bar when it opened at 10:00 the next morning, as were several of the professional drinkers, getting their head start for the weekend. Abbey was on time as well and we went to a table away from the mimosa and Bloody Mary drinkers. He set his briefcase on the table and took out several sheets of paper with numbers and text from top to bottom. He handed them to me and said, "Here's what you're looking for." I took the papers and pretended to be studying them when, in fact, I had no clue what I was looking at. Abbey was perceptive enough to figure that out, so he started explaining it to me. He said it took him a couple of hours to verify what he was seeing, but he was certain of his findings.

Old Herman was very adept at buying and selling commodities either just before, or just after some major news broke concerning that commodity. Herman would sell all his shares of Company A on Tuesday morning, while the stock was still riding high. Then Wednesday morning, Company A would announce they hadn't met their quarterly expectations, thus causing its share price to drop significantly. Conversely, Herman would buy a huge chunk of shares of Company B on Thursday. Then on Friday Company B would announce a major innovation to its business, causing its stock to skyrocket.

Old Herman was either a gypsy fortune-teller, or, he had someone (or several someones) giving him inside information. And trust me, old Herman was many things, but he was not a gypsy fortune-teller. It took me a couple of weeks to process this information and figure out what, if anything, I should do, or could do. What Herman was doing was illegal. People go to jail for long periods when convicted of "insider trading".

I didn't want Herman to get in trouble, in fact, I was happy with him. He was making me money month after month. But, knowing what I now did, I also knew Herman was making a lot of money on my investment. And I thought that I should get a higher percentage and Herman get a lower percentage of the money made off MY capital.

I set up a meeting with Herman. He was thinking I wanted to put more money in my account. I wasn't sure how to approach this with him. I finally figured it would be best just to come right out and get it on the table and go from there. His secretary brought us some coffee and when she left the room, Herman said, "How can I help you today George?" (I like it when people are trying to help me.) I told him, "Herman, I know what you're doing and I know how you're doing it and I don't care. I just want my fair share of the profits from MY investments. I don't care about all your other investments." He gave me his best "What in the world are you talking about?" look, and I repeated it to him again and said, "Do you want me to show you the proof?"

"There is no proof of anything" he said. "I have never done anything wrong and I am insulted by your accusations." Abbey had assured me that his hacking was undetectable. And in fact, he said Herman's company had a very antiquated system that most 12 year olds could probably get into. So, I brought out my proof. It wasn't iron-clad, but the timing of his buys and sells to the commodities rise and falls in the market were simply too coincidental to be just that—a coincidence. He looked at me and said I didn't know what I was talking about, that I had no clue how he ran his business. If I wanted to withdraw my money, he'd cut me a check right now.

"No Herman." I said, "I don't want to withdraw anything, and I don't want any of this information to ever become public knowledge. In fact, I want you to 'keep on keeping on.' But, I also know you're paying me a small percentage each month of my invested money. And I also know you personally are making a lot more than you're paying me on my investments, and I just want my fair share." He told me again, he was doing nothing illegal or unethical and that I could withdraw my funds anytime.

I got up and told him that I expected to see some increases in my next monthly statements. That's all. I didn't threaten him or hint at turning in my "evidence" to anyone. I just wanted my fair share of interest he was making on my money. Old Herman stopped seeing me for lunches and dinners and avoided me at social functions.

However, my monthly statements reflected a significant increase in my investments from his company. Thank you, Herman.

I had a long talk with myself on my next fishing trip about this turn of events. I read a passage in the Bible about "loving your neighbor" that really struck me; even forgiving someone 70 x 7 for something they did to you. I don't imagine what I did to old Herman would be forgivable in his eyes, even though he was a Deacon in the First Baptist Church. Was old Herman a "hypocrite" for doing what he was doing? Well, maybe so, but aren't we all? Show me any organization, school, church, family or gathering of any type which doesn't have hypocrites in their midst.

Humans are human. I've learned we all need forgiveness. The question I still can't seem to answer in my mind is: Will God forgive me for all I've done? Certainly I can't expect to lie, cheat and steal for an entire lifetime and then at the end simply ask to be forgiven and expect the same rewards as a deacon in the church (not Herman, but a good deacon). Can I? So I continue fishing, hoping I'll catch some answers to these questions, instead of catching a slimy, ugly catfish.

Everything in our lives seemed wonderful as we grew older. Amanda grew more beautiful with each passing year; whereas I started gaining weight around the middle. Not from beer drinking, but just lack of any physical exercise. Sitting in a boat all afternoon, trying not to catch fish does not qualify as an approved cardio exercise regimen. And, my hair seemed to be turning gray a lot faster than I thought it would. All of this bothers me a lot more than it does Amanda. She was only concerned that I exercise a little more for health reasons.

She was right, but I was just lazy—pure and simple, unlike my wife, who stayed busy and physically active. Amanda continued to do yoga and Pilates regularly. Then she started taking painting lessons at the local community college. Although, none of her paintings would probably sell on the open market, they were priceless to me and I kept them all forever. Later, she joined a women's hiking club and would go off to the Blue Ridge Mountains for day-long hikes. She was always full of energy and ideas with an apparent boundless enthusiasm for life. I fished.

I continued to keep tabs on my brothers. I heard from a friend of a friend of a friend that Teddy, and the latest woman he was living with, had moved to the beach and they were living in a camper her parents had left her. My friend wasn't sure if Teddy was working, but he was certain the lady was waiting tables at a breakfast restaurant there. My guess is, knowing my brother...he wasn't.

It never ceased to amaze me how Teddy could manipulate women and always find one who would support him and work for him. Although he was still woefully juvenile, Teddy had physically matured into a very handsome man. Full head of wavy hair the women simply adored. And somehow he doesn't ever seem to gain any weight, even though I seriously doubt he does any exercising, except maybe bending his elbow with a beer can. Yet, apparently, everyday is Margaritaville for my youngest brother. Good for him.

Frankie finally went to a rehab facility to help with his abuse issues. I found out he was now a live-in counselor at this place, helping others to overcome their various addictions. This was a complete surprise to me, I never envisioned Frankie helping anyone but himself. It just proves that people can change, maybe even me. Neither he nor Teddy have had any contact me with since the day I gave them the $5,000.

————

My business was still producing, investments had high yields and life was groovy. That is, until we got a call about 8:30 one night telling us that Amanda's parents had been in a car accident. And that it was serious. Whenever people their age are in an accident, it has to be serious. We rushed to the hospital and learned that their car had swerved into the other lane and hit a bus head on. Amanda's mom was most critical with multiple broken bones, cuts and internal injuries. Her dad had a broken arm and several cuts, including a nasty gash on his scalp. By morning, the doctors were telling us Amanda's mom was going downhill and it did not look good. She just had too many internal injuries.

Her dad was conscious, but in a lot of pain. He couldn't tell us, or the police, exactly what had happened. He did not remember anything except riding in the ambulance to the hospital. The police seemed to think he probably feinted, or had a momentary black-out which caused his car to cross lanes and hit the bus. The poor guy was in so much pain physically, and also emotionally because of what had happened to his wife, that he was barely coherent. Of course he blamed himself and there was no consoling him.

The doctors were right about Amanda's mom. Her injuries were so severe, she really had no chance. She died just after 11:00 the next morning. We were at the hospital where Amanda still worked, so everyone there tried their best to comfort Amanda and her dad. But what can you say at a time like this? You only have one mom, and they were very close. Her dad seemed to me to be in a state of shock. He wasn't crying or saying much of anything, he seemed sort of numb. Married for the great majority of your life to someone and then, without warning—they're gone. I couldn't imagine that.

He stayed in the hospital for a few days and was released to attend his wife's funeral. He was so sad. He didn't know what to say to anyone or what he should do. Without Amanda there, I'm sure he would have just crumpled up on the floor. It was hard. I felt helpless to do anything for my wife and I felt so badly for her dad. What would he do now? Could he continue living by himself? Should he come and live with us? Too many questions to answer now.

After the funeral, Amanda took an extended leave from work to take care of her dad. I urged her to retire, she didn't need to work any longer, we were financially set. She said she didn't want to make any decisions just yet. She'd wait and see what was going to happen with her dad. She spent most days with him, preparing meals, washing his clothes, cleaning the house—all the things her mom had always done.

He didn't feel like going out. His arm was bothering him and the cut on his scalp just didn't seem to be healing very well. A couple of weeks later he had an appointment at the doctor on Wednesday morning to be checked out and have the doctor look at the cut again. When Amanda got there to pick him up, he didn't answer the door. She opened it with her own key and found him still lying in his bed...dead.

They didn't do an autopsy. No need for that. The hospital staff said they really found no medical reason he should have died. I know why he died. If anything ever happened to Amanda, I'd die to. I understood it completely. So, within a three week period my lovely and caring wife had lost her mother and father. I only wished there was something I could do to help ease some of the pain and loss she was experiencing. As we all know, life is seldom fair. Good people get hurt, things happen which are unexplainable. Loved ones die. Bad people prosper and we all ask "Why?", when there is no answer available. It's life—the good, the bad and the ugly.

This took a lot out of Amanda. She felt best at the hospital, so she continued to work. Keeping busy kept her mind off all the tragic events that had happened. I tried to comfort her, but how can you comfort someone after all this? Her friends kept in constant contact and the neighbors brought us too much food. Frankie and Teddy even called her. They didn't want to speak with me. While Amanda went back to work, I instead, went to the lake on a Tuesday morning, which was unusual for me. I never missed work. I got in my boat and found a deserted spot, where I truly hoped no fish would visit.

I sat there and wondered about things, things I knew I would never find the answer to (in this world). But I still wondered. I never asked God why these tragic events happened...I knew why. I only asked Him to comfort my wife, the only person or thing I truly loved in the whole-wide world. My mission in life, from now on, was to make Amanda's life as enjoyable, loving, fun and wonderful as I possibly could.

After a couple of months, Amanda told me she wanted us to "get away" for awhile. Okay, exactly what did she mean by getting away? Selling her parents' house, disposing of all their furniture and possessions was a traumatic turn of events for her. She grew up in that house. Had her first kiss on the doorsteps of that house and she lived there throughout her high school and college years. It was not easy selling it to complete strangers. She finally sold it to a young couple with two children, who had recently moved here from Sparks, Nevada. She was happy the house would be full of life again.

Her parents left everything to Amanda in their Wills; and it was a lot. She knew I was doing some investing for her dad, but I cashed all that stuff out and told her to take the proceeds from everything and just hold onto it for awhile until she felt comfortable. If she ever felt comfortable doing anything with it. With the proceeds from the house, her parent's life insurance policies and stock investments, Amanda had a very healthy sum to just put into a savings account.

But that's what she did. To her, it was still her parent's money and she just couldn't do anything with it right now. I understood.

Okay, where did she want to go? Paris, London, Tokyo, Rome?

Wherever it was, I was going to take her, work would have to wait. But, she didn't want to go anywhere specific; she wanted us to pack some luggage in the car and take off. Great! "Where are we going?" I asked. She said "Nowhere and everywhere...wherever the road leads us. No plans, no maps, no destinations. We just start driving and see where it takes us." It's a weird feeling pulling out of your driveway and having no idea where you're going. Sort of like having dementia, and knowing you have dementia, but just not caring.

Before now, we were always going to work, to dinner, to a movie, to the lake, shopping, to the dentist, to Krispy Kreme (just me going there). The point is, you knew where to turn and where to stop. Today, I came to the first stop light and looked at Amanda. She shrugged her shoulders and I felt like a lost, little puppy, and I was only four blocks from my house

So, I drove. An hour or so later, she started humming a tune that I couldn't quite figure out. I knew it, but couldn't place it. It was bugging me so I finally had to ask her what it was..."In My Room" by the Beach Boys, she said. Then she sang it softly to me:

There's a world where I can go
And tell my secrets to
In my room
In this world I lock out
All my worries and my fears
In my room
Do my dreaming and my scheming lie awake and pray
Do my crying and my sighing laugh at yesterday
Now it's dark and I'm alone
But I won't be afraid
In my room

Then, she looked at me and said, "George, you're my room."

Somehow, we ended up in a westerly direction.

We crossed the Blue Ridge Mountains—spectacular as usual. Then we took some back roads and ended up that night in a Hampton Inn where the road intersected with Interstate 40.

After a breakfast of oatmeal and orange juice for Amanda and three eggs over easy, grits, toast, ham and home fries for me, we were on the road again. Yeah Willie, it's nice to be on the road again.

Through Tennessee we went, stopping at Elvis's house and taking the tour through Graceland with all the other wide-eyed groupies, junkies and devotees.

We stopped when we got tired and ate when we got hungry. Amanda told me not to worry about anything, including my diet, so I didn't. We saw a sign for the largest haystack in the world and we went there—it was a lot of hay. We drove the country and saw corn fields, soybean fields and all sorts of farmland. I had no clue what it all was, but somebody was working very hard.

We ate at Mom & Pops all across the Midwest. We had apple pies, peach cobblers and a rhubarb dessert (which tasted worse than it sounds). We tried everything from catfish on a stick to Aunt Maude's homemade sonkers, which were very good. I don't know what was in them, but they were good.

We passed through a bug storm in Arkansas, I actually had to turn the windshield wipers on to see the road the bugs were so thick. We drove through the barren, flat-lands of north Texas and made a stop in Paris, Texas; which obviously did not pattern itself after its namesake.

Onward through New Mexico where we stopped in Santa Fe for a couple of days, and loved it. It was sort of like a western, upscale hippie village.

Amanda bought some artwork, while I admired her artwork—if you know what I mean.

We passed through the Navajo Indian Reservation and ended up at Petrified Forest National Park, where I "borrowed" a piece of petrified wood from them. I fully intended to return it one day. We drove around Arizona, enjoying the red rock country near Sedona and ended up for the night in Flagstaff, Arizona.

I thought about looking at a map to see how far Winslow was from us, but I didn't.

We saw signs for the Grand Canyon, so off we went in search of the biggest hole in the world.

I'll never call it a hole again. Heck, I don't know what to call it, or how to describe it. I'm guessing that's why it's named the "Grand" Canyon.

All of the rooms at the canyon rim were booked, so we had to drive nearly all the way back to Flagstaff to find a room for the night. We were going back to the canyon the next day, then the next day, and then the next day.

We spent four awesome days there and saw light changing colors and textures and shapes that were simply indescribable. From there, we drove onward across the deserts, no goal in mind. Amanda said, "I think the country ends somewhere near here."

Well, I said, "Let's find out."

It did indeed end in a glorious place called Carmel-By-The-Sea.

We stopped at a couple of places in town and asked questions and directions. We eventually found what we were looking for: The Seven Gables Inn, the quaint, little bed-and- breakfast, which was owned by Seth's parents. (Our guide from the Pacific Crest Trail hike.) We stayed and wandered the beaches and little shops around Carmel and Monterey for several days. I don't actually remember how long we stayed there, because it seems like a dream now.

We crossed the Golden Gate Bridge...Why? By Gosh, because it was there!

No other reason. We kept driving northward through the magnificent redwood forests (we even drove through one of the redwood trees, which had a hole cut in it for cars to pass through). We passed Mt. Shasta and Mt. Rainier and kept on driving until some border guards wouldn't let us go any further. We understood, we really didn't care.

We then turned east and drove through beautiful country and marvelous little towns and cities. Twin Falls, Boise and Bozeman, where we met some real life cowboys in a cowboy bar.

These two young guys were the real deal. They were "yes sir and no ma'am" and as humble and proud and bowlegged as they could ever be. We were not the least bit disappointed when they told us they actually herded more sheep these days, than cattle. Yes Bob, "The times they are a'changing."

We rode in a hot air balloon over the Little Big Horn Battlefield and bought some arrowheads from a genuine Sioux Indian. At least he said he was, and then he said we could take his picture for $5. We declined the offer, since we didn't carry a camera with us on this adventure. But Amanda, being Amanda, gave him $5 anyway. My wife said no cameras. This trip would live in our hearts and minds only.

And it has.

We wandered the country for nearly six weeks. We had one flat tire, one bout of food poisoning in Dubuque, Iowa (from something called a salamander slider, which I just had to try), two bouts of constipation from all the riding, and a life time of memories that we'll never forget.

When we finally arrived back home, Amanda was ready to be home. The past was in the past and she was Amanda again.

25

After the trip, Amanda just didn't have it in her to return to work, I was thrilled. Now, I had her attention full-time. Financially, we were set for life, and I wanted us spend our remaining years focused on each other and enjoying life.

Soon after she retired she started bugging me to retire. At first, I could not envision anyone else ever running MY company. I built it up, grew it and nurtured it into a consistent money making enterprise.

I had even stopped taking cash into my private accounts. I didn't need it and the urge to always "have more" had unaccountably waned.

Everything was now above board and visible, and oddly enough, I was happy with that.

I pondered this change in my attitude when I went fishing. I know who I am, I know what I am, but somehow my perspective had been altered. Is it age? Is it contentment? Has God finally changed my heart? I didn't know the answers to these questions and sadly enough they went unanswered. As did the question I continued to ask over and over and over..."Jesus, can you ever forgive me for what I've done my entire life?"

Soon, I put out feelers for any buyers who might be interested in my company, hoping that no one would call me. But they did. A lot of them called. I'd become fairly close to our staff and over the years had substantially raised the salaries of them all. I didn't want anything to happen to their employment with new owners.

I narrowed down the list of potential buyers to those who were truly serious and those whom I liked. Some guys had great offers and excellent pedigrees, but I just didn't like them.

One team of prospective buyers came in and said they really wanted to make a competitive offer that I couldn't refuse. Okay, that sounded good to me. We talked and they did indeed have a fantastic offer; I was really starting to get excited.

After lunch, they wanted to just "walk around" and see the place, meet the people and get a feel for it. They'd only seen the financials so far. The actual warehouse was not that relative, in my opinion. I walked up front with the grayest-headed guy of the group, while his two subordinates walked behind us talking with each other. I soon started overhearing these two less-than-gray headed guys saying things like, "We can get rid of that..." and "We can change this..." and "We need to move this to our other site."

I finally stopped the tour, turned around and asked them "What are you two talking about?" "Well", they said, "We'll probably want to make some changes and integrate what you're doing here with our other locations." I looked at them, then back at the gray-headed guy, whose name was Dan, and said, "Dan, the tour is over. I think it's time you guys left." "Whoa", Dan replied, "We didn't mean anything, certainly didn't mean to make you mad. But you have to expect that any new owner is going to make changes". Well, maybe so, but I didn't expect to hear it. Not right in front of me and in my building, and it was still MY building, by God.

We smoothed things over a little—very little. But I had some thinking to do, some big thinking to do. I hadn't realized how much I loved this place. I didn't want it to change; I wanted it to stay just like this forever. I've always been a dreamer.

Eventually, after several offers from small investors to the big box people, I met a guy who came to see me by himself. He brought no briefcase and no papers. I don't even think he had a cell phone with him. His name was Bob Colvin, and I immediately liked old Bob. He was even older than me, but seemed full of life and his personality just bubbled over.

When I gave Bob a tour of the plant, all he wanted to do was meet each worker. He wanted to learn their names, ask how long they'd been working there and how many kids they each had.

Old Bob soon made friends with everyone there and remembered their names when we passed back through the plant later. He'd call out, "See you later Billy", "Nice meeting you Pedro", and "Take care of that cough Sandy." I knew Bob was the man to take over my company...if he had the money.

Well, old Bob had plenty of money. In fact, Bob was nearly a billionaire (that's with a "B"), but you'd have never known it. You'd have NEVER known it. I told Bob my concerns about changing the company and my concerns for the employees. He guaranteed me all employees would have a two year contract with him from the date of sale. He valued their experience and didn't want to lose any of them. But, he did say he would probably change some things, but only to increase business and hopefully add more jobs. That's why he bought businesses, he said.

I believed him.

The sale of my company went through pretty quickly. My last day as owner was a very sad one for me.

I told all the employees, most of whom had been with me since I bought the company, that I'd be back to visit. I knew I wouldn't. When it's gone, it's gone. Now, here I am with no company, no clinic, nothing left but a big pile of money. Poor, poor, pitiful me. What now George?

How are you going to enjoy your golden years? Heck, I'm not that old yet, I've got to find something or I'll drive Amanda crazy, or myself insane. I went out to the lake for the first week...just me, a cooler full of Pepsi's and Dr. Peppers, some crackers and a can or two of sardines. So far, retirement is looking good.

Amanda had a full slate of volunteer activities at the hospital. She should have just kept on working, at least she'd get paid for her time then. But, she didn't need the money, neither did I. In fact, I still had to figure out what to do with nine safe deposit boxes full of cash. I'd work on that later. Right now, God and I had a lot of things to discuss...starting with repentance. Dang, I wish a fish would bite my line. Please bite my line!

———————

Amanda could sense my restlessness around the house and one night out of the blue she said, "I think you should start playing golf. You'd like it." "What?" I said, "You cannot be serious, chasing a little ball around a field all day does not sound like the least bit of fun to me." She replied, "You can play by yourself. You can ride around in a little cart. You can take a cooler of beer with you. You'll see all sorts of birds and animals on the course and you don't even have to keep score if you don't want to. But if you do want to keep score, since you're playing by yourself, par can be whatever you want it to be. If you make a 9 on the first hole, since it's a par 10 on George's course, you just birdied that sucker!"

Amanda always had a way of making things look good. And, she always got her way. She'd already found a private club I could join and had made an appointment for me to meet the staff and club pro there at 9:00 the next morning.

Rolling Glen was a nice place with an extravagant clubhouse and a complete dining room and bar. It also had an exercise facility, a huge swimming pool and several larger rooms where they had social functions and dances from time to time. This golfing thing might be okay after all.

The dues were reasonable. The people were very nice and they brought me drinks and snacks while we talked. I think I could like these people. I then went to meet the club pro, his name was Harper Thompson III. He said to call him Harp, and I did. Harp asked me what my handicap was. I said besides being a tad old, color blind and conservative, I didn't really have one. "Hmm", he said, "What kind of clubs do you play with?" I pointed over to the corner of the pro shop at the shiniest set of clubs they had and said, "Those".

Well, good old Harp sold me some golf clubs, a golf bag, golf balls, a golf glove, a golf hat, golf shirts, golf pants and now declared I was an A-1 "golfer". "Harp" I said, "I don't see any woods in my new golf bag."

"There they are, driver, 3-wood and 5-wood." Harp said, as he pointed over to them. I said, "They're not made of wood anymore?" "Well, Mr. Kerry, they actually stopped making them out of wood about 40 years ago." "Oh, I guess I've got a lot to learn about golf." I'm sure old Harp either wanted to start laughing at me or start crying. I'm not sure which, but being the pro he was he just said, "I'll help you figure it out."

I did not want to totally embarrass myself at Rolling Glen, so I decided I would take golf lessons from Harp before I actually went on the course. At least I could learn how to hold these sticks and learn the proper etiquette. I made my mind up I wouldn't play on the course until I could at least hit the ball on a regular basis, with some idea of which direction it would go. Nope, I'd stay in the practice area and let old Harp teach me everything he could.

After six weeks with Harp, I finally felt as though I might be able to birdie the first hole, which Amanda had already told me was a par 10.

I got my tee time in mid-afternoon, when no one else was playing, so I could be all by myself and experience the fruits of my labor in golden solitude. Harp wished me well and told me to "Have fun." Well Harp, what else was I expected to have? Okay, I'll try. Have fun George, have fun.

Please have fun. And I did until I hit my virginal tee shot on the first golf hole I ever played.

I topped it and it rolled about twenty yards and stopped on the women's tee. Dang! I drove up there and as I was preparing to hit the second golf shot of my life, some snerky teenager on the practice tee over to the side, yells at me and says, "Hey sir! That's the women's tee. The senior tee is back there." Have fun George. Have fun.

Well, I'll have you know, I made it to the green and had a putt for a double eagle. But I left it just short and tapped in for an eagle 8. I was as proud as I've ever been of anything. I then bent over and reached down to pick up my ball from the cup. The next thing I remember, I woke up in a hospital room. Buzzers going off, wires taped all over my chest, nurses doing whatever it is nurses do, and Amanda standing next the bed, holding my hand and crying.

When Amanda saw me wake up, she ran out of the room and immediately came back with a guy who looked like he was in high school. Except he had a doctor's coat on with a nametag that said "Dr. Dalton." He asked me several questions about how I felt and what I remembered. I answered "I feel lousy and I don't remember anything". It seemed like I couldn't catch my breath for some reason. I said, "What happened to me?" He said, "Mr. Kerry, you've had a massive heart attack, your heart stopped twice on the way to the hospital. We're going to take you into surgery immediately and do at least a quadruple by-pass, but we'll know more when we get in there."

I looked at Amanda and she started crying harder, so hard that she couldn't talk. She could only hold my hand with both of hers. She started wailing, "It's all my fault. I made him play golf, I almost killed him!" "Whoa honey, it's definitely not your fault. First of all, I'm not dead. Second, I enjoyed my one hole of golf, and third, if anyone is to blame here, it's me and Mr. Krispy Kreme." Dr. Dalton then came back in with a clipboard and asked the nurses to leave the room. He wanted to talk with us in private. I could tell by his demeanor, this was not going to be something I wanted to hear, and I didn't.

He said I came as close to dying on the golf course as anyone he's ever seen. It was only the quick actions of some teenagers, coming to my rescue when they saw me fall, giving me CPR, and calling 911 immediately that saved my life.

Maybe they weren't so snerky. Then came the bad news. He had consulted with other cardiologists and surgeons on staff and they all came to the same conclusion. They felt if they went ahead and operated immediately, I might have around a 20% chance of survival. If they waited even one more hour, I'd be dead. My heart was so damaged they weren't sure it would keep beating for even one more hour.

They wanted us to know how serious it was and what the results would likely be. Amanda had begged them to be honest with us, and they were. Dr. Dalton said he was going to prep for the operation and they would give me and Amanda about 15 minutes alone before they came back to get me. Just in case we needed time to get any affairs in order. I was stunned! One moment I'm playing golf; the next moment I'm going into surgery with an 80% chance of dying.

Truly, I was not scared for myself, but Amanda kept saying over and over, "It's all my fault, it's all my fault." I thought, "Okay George, you've got about ten minutes left. You'd better make the best of it."

My brain was swirling. When you might only have 10 minutes left to live, EVERYTHING crosses your mind. I told Amanda I loved her more than anything in the world, more than life itself. If the Lord took me right now, I'd feel I was blessed to have spent all these years with the most beautiful, wonderful, loving woman in the world. This only made her cry harder. I knew Amanda was well taken care of financially, between what her parents left her and her own savings, she would be considered "rich". Plus, the life insurance policy on my life and all my accounts and savings and investments would put her into the very top financial category—not that she cared about any of that.

"Five minutes left George. Do I tell her about all the safe deposit boxes or not? If I die and don't tell her, no one will ever know about the money." I paid for the boxes in advance for 25 years so they wouldn't ever send any statements to our house. I never actually counted the money in all of them, but I did count one box and they were all about the same size. The one I counted had nearly $150,000 in it. I'm sure the other eight were close, if not more. These were the BIG boxes.

I decided I had to tell her. I couldn't let over a million dollars just disappear. I said, "Amanda, I have something to tell you that you're not going to understand. Just let me finish telling you before you ask any questions. Okay?" "Yes" she said, "But hurry the nurses will be here any minute."

As quickly as I could, I told her about the safe deposit boxes and where the keys were. Her name was always on the account so she could access them in case anything happened to me. I gave her a quick overview about where the money came from. In two minutes I told her about Mike, about the cash from my business, about the clinic, about Nicky. I would've told her everything if the nurses had not come back in the room. Amanda looked at me with a totally blank expression on her face, too stunned to speak. As they started rolling me out I called to her "Amanda? Amanda? Amanda..." As the nurses got my rolling bed out of the room and into the hallway to start for the operating room, Amanda walked to the doorway, looked at me and said, "I thought I knew you. I don't."

They had started some sort of IV in my arm. The medicine, or anesthesia from the tubes knocked me out before I even got to the operating room. The only thing I remember was the pained and hurtful expression on Amanda's face and those terrible words I'll never forget. "I thought I knew you. I don't." Obviously, I survived the operation, which was indeed a quadruple by-pass with all sorts of other technical, medical jargon thrown in. Who cares?

When I finally woke up in the recovery room, I was alone. Amanda was not there. Some young nurse, who was busy filling out some charts, told me a lady had come to my room when they brought me out of surgery. When the doctors told her the operation was a success, she had leaned over and whispered something to me. Then she walked out. This nurse didn't know what Amanda had whispered in my ear. I asked her if visitors were allowed in. She said, "Of course they are." But there were no visitors, I was alone. At that point, I wished I hadn't survived. I wished I was dead, but I wasn't. I was just alone. That was worse than being dead.

I stayed in the hospital for eight days and had one visitor, Bob Colvin, the guy who bought my company. I tried calling home. No answer. I called Amanda's cell phone. No answer. When they released me I called a taxi to pick me up and take me home. What would I say to her when I walked in the door? How could I ever make this right between us? Unfortunately for me, I didn't have to confront any of those questions. She was gone.

All her clothes and personal possessions were gone and nothing was left but an empty shell, full of heartbreaking memories and a letter on the kitchen cabinet. The letter read, "George, don't try to contact me. Please, I'm begging you. Don't contact me." That's all. Not where she'd gone, not what she was thinking, not what was going to happen between us... nothing, but "...Don't contact me."

I couldn't stay here alone. I was too weak to do anything for myself. I had no one to call. I didn't even try to call either of my brothers. I'm pretty sure they would never help do anything except make things worse. No, here I was with a nice house and all the money I would ever need, and totally, completely alone. I called the taxi back to pick me up again and take me to the Hyatt downtown. I knew I could order room service and they would change the sheets and towels while I lay in bed trying to get my strength back. The doctor's gave me a strict diet. What did I care? The first night there I ordered a cheeseburger, fries and a banana split.

I called a private investigation company the next morning. It took them about 45 minutes to find that Amanda had gone back to Manassas. She had some aunts and uncles there and some old college friends. I wouldn't contact her (as she wished), but I had to know she was okay. I stayed in the Hyatt for nearly three weeks before I decided to move out. I thought about going back home, but it wasn't a home anymore.

I decided to leave it as it was in case Amanda somehow decided to return. I left all the furniture in the house and I left all the power and heat on. The only thing I stopped was the paper and the mail. After a couple of weeks I contracted a cleaning company to go in the house every two weeks and clean the place from top to bottom, just in case Amanda came back.

I found a furnished condo near the lake and moved in there. It was nice, two bedrooms, two baths, nice view of the lake. But it wasn't home. It never would be. I had my boat there and most days I'd go out on the lake. Sometimes I'd even take a fishing pole (with no bait). Whereas, in the past, my conversations were with God, now, most of my conversations were a one-way dialogue with Amanda. I talked to her hours and days on end—week after week—month after month—lifetime after lifetime. I mixed in a few conversations with God. I didn't blame Him. All this happened because of me; because of the things I did. Because I am who I am.

I stayed in the condo for over two years and didn't receive one phone call, or one letter from Amanda. I kept tabs on her, not out of jealousy, only to make sure she was okay and didn't need anything. The guy who owned the private investigation company, Joe, did a thorough job. As far as I know Amanda never knew he was checking up on her. She eventually started doing volunteer work at the hospital there in Manassas. She'd go to the movies with some friends. She visited New York occasionally, and she spent holidays with her aunts and uncles and their families.

She bought a new car and moved into a condo of her own near her aunt's house. She was safe and comfortable. Joe told me everything about her, except if she was happy. Except if she would ever come back to me. Except if she still loved me. And, most importantly, if she would ever forgive me.

Joe took a personal interest in me, I'm not sure if it's because I paid him so well, or he just didn't have any other business at the time. I also think he felt sorry for me. Joe was a retired Military Policeman, with over twenty years of service. He'd had his Private Detective license for almost eleven years now. He had a wife and five kids and was now experiencing his second fatherhood as most of his children were presenting him with grandchildren. I think it made Joe feel badly to see me all alone, with no wife, no kids, no family, no friends...nothing. When he would report back to me, he always hung around and talked. Not about business, but what one human being would do for another human being who was in pain. Joe was a good man.

I could never forgive myself for what I'd done to Amanda. I didn't care about anything any longer. My portfolio continued to grow and I simply didn't care. I even cleaned out one of the safe deposit boxes and split the money in half, wrapped it up in plain white paper and stuffed it into two boxes. I had Joe address one box to Frankie and the other to Teddy. I didn't want them seeing my handwriting on the packages. I had him drive up to Pennsylvania and mail each box to them, with no return address and a postmark from a location

214

they wouldn't recognize. There was no note inside, just $75,000 in cash for each of my brothers. That's a good indication of the depth of my despair.

I then put a hundred dollar bill in an envelope. No note, just the $100. I sealed it and asked Joe to find a Mobley Morrison from my hometown, my age, and give him this envelope. Don't answer any questions, just give him the envelope and walk away. If Mobley is not alive, then give it to someone in his family. Joe may have thought this was odd behavior, but I was paying him very well not to think, just to do as I wished. He indeed found Mobley, gave him the envelope and walked away. He said Mobley, and his wife, were having a cup of coffee in their home when he knocked on the door. Mobley was a little overweight and pretty bald, but other than that, he looked good... I was glad to hear that.

He told me Mobley took the envelope, said, "Thank you" and shut the door. He did report that someone pulled the shades back on a window to check him out as he drove away, but other than that, it was a clean and simple operation. I then had Joe take the piece of petrified wood I had borrowed, package it up and mail it to the Petrified Forest National Park in Arizona. No return address.

Still no word from Amanda. Not that she wanted a divorce. Not that she hated my guts. Not that she wanted me dead and most importantly, not that she forgave me. However, I would never give up hope. Never. Never. Never. You only meet the love of your life once...only once. Nothing else matters and no one else matters.

Soon, my condo on the lake started feeling like a prison. Nothing in life was enjoyable any longer. Movies were boring. Dinners were bland and uninspiring and television was insufferable. I got restless and started moving around. I rented a condo at Virginia Beach for six months (the least amount of time they would lease one to me). I walked on the beaches there. I fished some off the pier. I sat out on the beach and watched families and lovers and friends enjoy each other, but I could only think of what I had lost.

I remembered my fistfight not far from where I now sat. I remembered rubbing lotion on Amanda's back and finding sea shells to give to her—and the way she would laugh and giggle. I remembered just staring at her as she napped, thinking this was the most beautiful creature God ever made. I thought all these things, and more, until I had to leave. It was too painful.

I rented an apartment in New York City for about nine months, I revisited all the places Amanda loved to go, it was not the same without her there. Nearly every day I would go to the same upscale coffee shop and buy an overpriced cup of coffee. After several months I almost got used to the taste of it. However, I didn't go for the coffee. I went because it was near the spa Amanda loved to visit. One cold morning I had my paper in hand and neared the door to the coffee shop, almost looking forward to my premium, fancy cup of coffee. I looked in the window and saw Amanda standing in line with another woman.

They were laughing at something, I couldn't tell if they were friends, there together, or just two strangers making conversation in line at a coffee shop. I backed up to the corner of the window, pulled my hat down low and watched the love of my life, the love of my existence, pay for a cup of coffee and turn around. I walked away before she could see me. I did not want to ruin her day, or life, any more than I already had. It may have seemed strange, even for New Yorkers, to see an old man walking down the street sobbing like a baby, but that is what they saw if they looked my way.

For a few more months, I went back to the coffee shop every day.

I read the paper. I drank lousy coffee and watched all the people coming and going. But I never saw Amanda again. I eventually got tired of the cold and moved to Miami for nearly a year. Do you see the pattern here? I was going back to the places where Amanda and I had great times, trying to relive those memories, trying to forget the present, trying to forgive myself. Trying. Trying. Trying.

In Miami I ate a lot of Cuban food which gave me indigestion and heartburn. Even though I stopped eating it so often, I was still having stomach issues. I'd have to get that checked out soon. I decided I'd fly to San Francisco, rent a car and drive down to Carmel-by-the-Sea and stay at the same bed and breakfast Amanda and I stayed at all those years ago. On the flight, I really felt sick to my stomach, and I just kept feeling bad all the way to Carmel.

As soon as I checked in, I went to the bathroom and that's when I found blood in my urine. The next day, there was blood in my urine and stool. I knew this wasn't good. I tried to stay a little longer, but I just felt terrible. So, I booked a flight back home to Virginia, where my doctors were. That's when I got the cancer news, Wednesday, July 23. You never forget the day you find out you're going to die.

Having no one to call, or at least lacking anyone who would really care about my condition, I decided to stop at "Dubliners," an Irish bar, and see if I could unload my troubles on the bartender. At 11:00 in the morning, there weren't many people in the bar that woeful Wednesday. All the tables were empty and I didn't want to make the bartender walk away from the bar. I saw an open seat at the far end and sat next to where a Catholic priest was sitting by himself, nursing something tall, black and foamy. The bartender was busy either telling jokes, or making moves on a pretty, young, college-aged girl sitting at the other end of the bar. I couldn't tell what he was saying, but she was giggling and laughing at whatever he was spinning.

He soon ambled down my way and asked what I wanted, "Cape Cod" I replied, "I was there once with my wife and I'd like to remember that little trip now." I just couldn't let it go. "Coming right up," he said, "and how are you doing, Father?" I started to get smart with him and tell him I wasn't his father, nor did I want to be. But, before I could put my foot completely in my mouth, the priest spoke up said, "I'm fine for now Danny. Thanks for asking."

Then, the priest asked me how I was doing. Well George, here's your chance to unload all your troubles and sins and concerns and all your lifetime full of regrets and sorrows on a man of the cloth. It's his job to listen, isn't it? I turned to look at him and took a deep breath, but only said, "Great, I hope you are." I think he could tell that wasn't entirely accurate. He asked my name and in some sort of Irish/Scottish/English accent, told me his was Keiland. I said, "Well, do I call you Keiland or Father Keiland?" He said Keiland was just fine for the time being. He was a fairly young guy I think, maybe around 32 or 33, but my perception of the ages of people seems to be a bit skewered as I've aged. I said, "I don't think you're from around here are you Keiland?" "Quite perceptive, George," he replied, "I'm actually from Ireland, County Kerry to be precise."

I'd never met an Irishman before and was intrigued by his accent.

And I wondered why a priest was sitting in a bar at 11:05 on a Wednesday morning. It almost made me forget about my own troubles. So, having nothing to lose, I asked him why he was in the bar this morning. He told me that after performing early mass at eight o'clock, he was officially on vacation and was leaving tonight on a flight back to Ireland for two blessed weeks. Having no knowledge whatsoever of Ireland, or this County Kerry he was referring to, I asked him about his homeland. What was it like? I said, "Doesn't it rain a lot over there Keiland?" He replied, "George, you don't go to Ireland for the sunshine." I didn't know what that meant, but somehow, it made perfect sense.

He then said, "George, any Kerryman, like myself, will tell you that there are only two kingdoms: the Kingdom of God and the Kingdom of Kerry. One is not of this world and the other is out of this world." All I could do was look at him and smile, probably the first smile I've truly had in many weeks. I asked him why he was here, in Virginia, and not home in Ireland? Seemed like a tame question.

This is what he told me.

"When I was a young priest, my parrish adopted a stray cat that just had kittens. One day, something scared one of the kittens and it climbed up a small tree in front of the church. The little kitten was too scared to climb back down the tree and had climbed too far up for me to reach, and the tree limbs were too small for me to climb. In all my priestly wisdom, I decided to throw a rope up around one of the branches, then tie the rope to my car and gently pull the top of the tree downward until I could reach the stranded kitten.

My plan worked to perfection. The tree started bending slowly downward, slowly downward. I stopped, got out of my car and saw that maybe two or three feet more and I would be able to reach the scared, little kitten. I got back in and just as I let off the brake, BOING! The rope broke. The tree flung itself back upwards like a slingshot, sending the little kitten off into space.

I jumped out of the car and looked around but could not find the kitten anywhere. Obviously, God had decided to take this little kitten home. After a few minutes of reflection, I recovered. After all, it was just a little kitten. We had 5 or 6 others. The next week, I'm visiting one of my parishioners and notice they have a new dog pen. They'd never penned their dog up before. I thought this was a little strange, so I asked them why they started fencing in their dog. Mrs. McShane told me their little girl, Muirran, had been pestering them every week for a kitten—nothing else. All she wanted was a little kitten.

Well, the McShanes were dog people, always had been and had no intention of getting their little daughter a kitten. But, to soothe her daughter, Ms. McShane told her if she truly wanted a kitten, then she should pray to God and maybe He would provide one for her. So, every night little Muirran would say her prayers, always ending them with the hope of a little kitten. A few days later, Mr. McShane was taking Muirran for a ride in his horse drawn carriage on the road in front of the church and miraculously, out of nowhere, a kitten drops into the carriage from out of the sky. What choice did they have? God had provided the kitten. Now, all they could do was pen up the dog." He continued... "George, I am that kitten. Slung from Ireland to Virginia because somebody here prayed to God for an honest priest...and here I am."

I think—no, I know I believe him. You can't make up something like that. After a few minutes of me staring at him, he finally said, "George, I feel you want to ask me something. Do you?" It was senseless pretending, so I said, "I do Keiland, I have several things I'd like to ask, if you have the time." He said, "George, we have an eternity." I gave him the short, compact version of my life. That I'd been diagnosed with cancer and it didn't look good for me. That my wife had left me because of my scandalous past, and I also told him about my fishing trips where I kept asking God questions, searching for answers.

Keiland talked and I listened, I asked a few questions and he listened. Being a priest, I asked him what surprised him most about people. He said, "That they will lose their health to make money, then lose their money to restore their health." More often in America than in Ireland, but not exclusively. He also told me he was surprised that most of the people he knew here in Virginia lived neither in the present nor the future. But, they lived as if they would never die. I had the distinct impression Keiland was looking in my heart and describing my life. I asked him what lessons he would like me and others to learn that could help us in our lives. He said, "I'd like for you to learn that it's not good to compare yourselves to others, George. A rich man is not the one who has the most money, but he's the one who needs the least."

I was mesmerized, almost transfixed, by the wisdom in this 33 year old transplanted Irishman. I asked him what other lessons he would like me to learn. He responded, "To learn that it only takes a few seconds to open profound wounds in people we love, but, it takes many years to heal them." He continued,

"And, I'd like everyone to learn that two people can look at the same thing and see it differently."

I didn't know what else to say, but I knew if I asked any more questions, I'd end up sobbing in my untouched Cape Cod. I was astounded by Keiland's words and his wisdom. I told him I had to be going and wished him a great trip to Ireland later that night. I then told the bartender to bring my tab and Keiland's as well. Buying him a drink was the least I could do. As I got up from the stool, Keiland grabbed my arm and said, "There's one more lesson I'd like you to learn George, and it's an important one." "Okay, I'm listening." He looked deeply in my eyes and said, "I want you to learn that it's not always enough to be forgiven by others. That first, you must forgive yourself."

The bartender came back and gave me my change, $42. I looked at the money knowing I only gave him a twenty to pay for the two drinks. Every other day in my life, I would have pocketed that money and walked out the door whistling "Dixie". Not today. I told him he made a great mistake and gave all the money back and told him to"Keep the change". I turned around to tell Keiland goodbye again, but the barstool was empty. He was gone.

I started my hospital visits the next day. The doctor started me on all sorts of medicines; then radiation and chemotherapy treatments. None of it seemed to make much difference. The cancer would

223

appear to be in remission for a month or two, then suddenly explode on my next visit. The treatments made me sick and nauseous and feeling weak all the time. The only thing they didn't do was make my hair fall out. Somehow, I kept a full head of silvery hair. It was just everything else that fell apart.

So, here I am now, dying, wasting away and totally alone. My secretary, who's recording this sad story, who had yet to ever ask me a question or comment about anything, did in fact ask me a question this morning. She hemmed and hawed around, beating around the bush, and I finally said, "Spit it out, ask me whatever you want. It's okay." She looked directly in my eyes and asked, "How does it feel knowing you're going to die?" Her name was Vicki, no "e" at the end (but no heart dotting the "i" either). I tried to think of something profound to tell her, but I couldn't think of anything. I could only say.

"In my case Vicki, it's not unwelcome." I should've just shut up at that point and left that poor girl alone, but I didn't. I couldn't.

"When you're all alone, as I am, and you've lost the only thing in the world that's important to you, then nothing else matters. What's the point of going on? What's the point of getting up in the morning when you have nothing to live for? I want to go face God and confess my sins to Him face-to-face, and see if what I've been reading all these years is true: that He will forgive me and love me."

Several moments passed and Vicki's gaze never left mine. You know, it's difficult to look someone directly in the eyes for very long without looking away. At this moment, with Vicki, it wasn't hard. It was as though I couldn't look anywhere else. Vicki then broke the silence and said, "I think you need to confess those sins BEFORE you die." Then she said, "And, Mr. Kerry, you need to do that with your wife as well."

Of course, Vicki was right. I'd already asked God a million times to forgive me. But Amanda asked me not to contact her, and I hadn't. I knew I didn't have much time left. I was getting weaker every day and sleeping most of the time. I stopped taking any medications except the stuff they gave me for pain. Those pills were the only friends I had left in the world now. But, the more I thought about Vicki's comment, the more sense it made to me. I asked her to get me a piece of paper and pen. She propped me up in bed and I wrote this,

"Amanda, I love you more than anyone has ever loved anything in the history of the world. I did wrong. 'Sorry' cannot describe how I feel. I'm dying now. Do you think it's possible you can ever forgive me? Love, George"

I had Joe, my private investigator, take this note to Manassas and tape it to the door on Amanda's condo. Then wait outside, in his car, to make sure she actually received it. When he returned, he told me she took the note off the door, opened it and read it on her front porch. He couldn't tell exactly, but he thought she may have started crying. He wasn't sure. Then she opened the door and went inside.

225

I know it's near the end now, I'm only conscious for short periods at a time. I keep asking God to forgive me, but how will I know if He forgives me? Someone has made the decision to have a hospice nurse with me 24 hours a day now. I don't know who did that, but it must mean they know I only have a day or two left. I can't seem to open my eyes any longer. I don't really want to. It's peaceful just lying here. I can't really tell, but I don't think I'm moving my arms or legs either and I know I'm not verbally speaking. It's only my thoughts now. However, I can hear the nurse. I hear her moving around. I hear her phone conversations and the toilet flushing. It's almost surreal now how these noises have intensified.

I have no idea if its day or night, but I seem to have been asleep for quite some time. I think I'm still alive. I don't feel as though I'm dead yet, but I feel perfectly at peace. I hear a voice, but I can't tell if it's a man or a woman. It's just a voice. I think I feel someone touching my hand, I'm not really sure. Even though I'm trying as hard as I can to identify the words I'm hearing, I can't seem to make them out. I feel like I'm slowly fading away, almost like floating into a cloud. It's not unpleasant. In fact, it's reassuring. Then, I heard the last words I ever heard on earth, clearly and distinctly. I just don't know who said them...

"George, I forgive you."

EPILOGUE

George's company did very well under the leadership of Bob Colvin. He soon took the company public and the stock immediately began to rise. Old Herman called Bob several times trying to set up a lunch meeting with him, but Bob was on a healthy diet. He simply could not afford to let Herman's fast food menu jeopardize his life or affairs.

Pam Woods met the love of her life on the internet.

She had a successful career and invested the money she made from the clinic very wisely. She was able to retire early and move to Sausalito, California, where she and the love of her life have lived a long, loving, prosperous life together.

CJ eventually met someone who understood him. They got married and seemed to be very happy, yet, he never did have any children. He sold a huge amount of insurance however, and has season tickets to all football, basketball and baseball games. His first wife remained a little plain and plump, but, ended up marrying four other guys after CJ.

Rudy and his partner stayed in Asheville. Rudy continued working at the hospital there, and they also opened a wine bar downtown that specializes in sweet, fruity wines. Tim stayed at the clinic, brought his fiancé to the U.S. and eventually had six beautiful and talented children. Gabriel left the clinic after he'd made a substantial amount of money. He moved back to Kansas City, where he works as a part-time consulting doctor at the hospital and as a full-time session guitar player for the local recording industry.

No one ever heard from Mike again. He simply disappeared. Richie was caught in an illegal diamond importing scheme. He lost his business and most of his assets. His beauty pageant wife left him and he spent a few months in jail. While in prison, he fell in love with the assistant warden, supposedly the most attractive woman in the prison system. They married when Richie was released and are living happily in her old house, with two cats in the yard.

Dana made a zillion dollars. Elizabeth married a professional golfer, who now plays on the senior tour, and is a member of Pinehurst Country Club. Janet and Charles lived a wonderfully full life—entertaining and exciting in all facets...except maybe the bedroom. Julie only had the twins, no other children. Her husband died early from a heart attack and left her a lot of money. She takes two or three cruises each year, usually to different destinations and always with different guests accompanying her.

Bea married the president of the local YMCA and her three children all graduated from college; one from the University of Virginia, one from Georgetown, and the youngest daughter from Salem College. They each obviously inherited their mother's intelligence.

Emily led a charmed life. She married a writer and later became an author herself of romance novels. She even had one book turned into a Lifetime movie.

Nicky was always Nicky.

A few months before George died, he had his investigator, Joe, drive him to all the banks around town where he emptied out all his safe deposit boxes. He had Joe buy a dozen or so big travel bags—the expensive ones with locks on them. George would go into the bank alone and empty all the cash into a travel bag and close the account. He did this for each and every one. Joe didn't ask questions, or know what was in the bags. He may have suspected, but he truly had no idea, and George never told him.

Knowing that Amanda was already very wealthy, and that she would never touch this "dirty money."

George told Joe he wanted him to either mail, or deliver, each of the travel bags after his death, to the following people, with explicit instructions on how to deliver each bag.

Here's what George sent to each of these people:

For Frankie: $150,000 mailed to him from somewhere in Tennessee, with no return address. There was no note in the bag. It contained nothing but hundred dollar bills.

For Teddy: $150,000 mailed to him from somewhere in North Carolina, with no return address. There was also no note in the bag, only the money.

$100,000 each for Tim, Gabriel and Rudy, with an anonymous note on the inside thanking them for being great and wonderful men.

For Keiland: $100,000, with a note from "a friend" telling him to "dance with the fairies and leprechauns" and keep teaching people life's lessons.

Joe tried to deliver the money in person, but both Catholic churches in town told him they'd never heard of a priest named Keiland. Joe is still investigating.

For Janet: $100,000 and a six-pack of Pabst Blue Ribbon. No note.

For Bea: $100,000 with an anonymous note that read, "For one of the best women I ever knew."

For Emily: $100,000 and a book of poetry. No note.

For Elizabeth: one Virginia Commonwealth University tee shirt. No money, no note.

For Dana: no money, no note. Just these ten books delivered to her:

For Whom the Bell Tolls

Grapes of Wrath

To Kill a Mockingbird

Black Sun

Anna Karenina

All Quiet on the Western Front

Brass Verdict

Firefly Lane

Naked Prey

Rough Country

For Vicki: $25,000 for having no "heart" over the "i" in her name, but instead, having a caring and insightful heart of her own.

The last travel bag was for Joe. It contained the remainder of the cash from all the safe deposit boxes George had accumulated all these years, $111,700, and a note thanking him for being a good friend and a good man.

———

Frankie took the $150,000 he anonymously received in the mail and started his own rehab facility for veterans who were experiencing symptoms of PTSD. Soon, state and federal grants poured in as well and Frankie was making a name for himself as one of the most admired leaders in the state. Senators, congressmen, lawyers and all sorts of politicians competed with each other for the right to be photographed and filmed with Frankie at the rehab clinic.

Teddy took his $150,000 and bought a small house trailer on the Outer Banks of North Carolina at Ocracoke Island. He spends most of his days fishing and drinking margaritas. His current live-in girlfriend (20 years younger than him), works her shift at the ticket counter for the ferry that runs between Ocracoke and the main land. He is living his dream.

Amanda never recovered from her broken heart. The love of her life came only once as well. She remained single and beautiful all the rest of her days.

And George...Yes, he was forgiven.

About the Author

This is the first novel written, after four previous works of non–fiction, by Gary R. Hope. When asked why he switched suddenly from non–fiction to fiction writing, he responded: "Because change gives me an opportunity to think, and lets my imagination take me anywhere I want to go."